JESSICA

Helena Hann-Basquiat

with

J.S. Collyer Michelle Combs

Freya McMillan Hayley Morgan

Lizzi Rogers Hannah Sears

dilettante publishing

Jessica
Copyright © 2014, Helena Hann-Basquiat

ISBN 13: 978-0-9940419-2-0
ISBN 10: 0-9940419-2-6

Published in Canada by Dilettante Publishing

JESSICA

JESSICA

S he's gone," I cried, running carelessly up the creaky basement stairs. If I wasn't careful, I could trip and break my neck.

"Who?" Penny asked. My niece had been ignoring my frantic behaviour for the past half hour, but she finally broke her silence.

"Jessica," I said. "She's just... *gone*."

There are rumours that I keep a writer trapped in my basement, chained to a chair, writing stories by candlelight in her own blood on dirty yellowed parchment, but I assure you, those rumours are exaggerations, darlings. Jessica is and always was here of her own free will. She's a strange one, I'll give you that, but I didn't abuse her. You have to believe me.

"Where would she go?" Penny wondered. "I mean, does she have any family, or friends, or..."

I looked at Penny as if to ask what she was thinking, or rather, to remember who she was talking about.

"Right," she shrugged. "But, you've got to admit, Helena, you don't know much about her."

"No, you're right," I agreed. "But why would she just leave?"

"Why did she come to you in the first place?" Penny countered.

It was a dark and stormy night. No, really.

There was so much thunder that I almost didn't hear the pounding.

I opened the door and there she was, soaking wet, her long black hair almost completely concealing her face. Her clothes – barely recognizable as such, hung off her in tatters, and the skin that showed through was marbled with the red, purple and yellow of violent bruises. In her hands, she clutched a ragged old rucksack that looked like it had been through wars.

"Help me," she cried, her voice sounding like the raven from that Poe story, and passed out on my doorstep.

I took her in without thinking, and nursed her back to health. She didn't speak a word for months, and when I tried to call someone for help – the police or a hospital, she threw a terrifying fit, screaming without words, wailing like a banshee, and tearing at her own skin until it bled. I don't know why I let her stay, but she'd been with me ever since, and whether she was running from something she'd done, or hiding from something that hunted her, I was never really sure.

"So who is she, though?" Penny asked. We'd avoided talking about Jessica. I suppose I just never really wanted to know. I admit, she kind of frightened me.

"I don't really know," I said. "She didn't have any I.D. on her, and the only name she gave me was Jessica – I added that B. Bell stuff later when I started publishing her writing. I don't know her real last name – and you want to know what's weird? I don't think *she* does, either."

"What do you mean?"

"Well, whatever it was that happened to her – whatever brought her to my doorstep – it must have been truly awful. She's never spoken of it, of course, but I get the feeling whatever happened to her, well, it might be happening still."

"Do you think people are looking for her?" Penny asked in alarm.

I shrugged. "I don't know."

"Well, did she take all her things? Maybe she left a note or something?"

I looked at Penny again and shrugged. Jessica didn't have much in the way of possessions.

"I found this," I said, holding up a beat up old book. It was leather bound and looked very old. I flipped through it and saw a couple different peoples' handwriting, as well as newspaper clippings, and what looked like excerpts from a medical report.

"What is it?" Penny asked. "Do you think it's hers?"

"Must be," I said.

"Well, what's it say?"

JESSICA

From the Journal of Dr. Kenneth Howard, Psy.D., M.D.

March 14, 1974

I have decided to keep this journal for the sake of my own understanding, and nothing more. I have no intention of sharing these thoughts with anyone in a professional capacity, but should anything happen to me, and this journal is found, perhaps the contents here will aid in any investigation into my death or disappearance.

First, I have no idea what happened to the child. As of the time of this writing, I have no knowledge of her whereabouts, or indeed, whether the poor creature even still lives, for her very birth defies science. If I were a religious man, I would say that her existence is something of a blasphemy, but I will try to contain my thoughts to a less superstitious way of thinking, though to be honest, I am truly at a loss.

It was the girl's mother with whom I was acquainted. She was a patient of mine, referred to me by a colleague at Miskatonic University who was studying abnormal psychology and the physiology of the brain. My patient – I'll call her Margo for sake of anonymity – was participating in a study on migraines. Using cutting-edge technology like Magnetic Resonance Imaging and Computer Assisted Tomography, my colleague Dr. West was monitoring brain activity during migraine attacks, and recording the effects of various administered drugs on the patients. Mostly beta-blockers like propranolol and metoprolol, as I understand it, though he was also experimenting with varying doses of botulinum toxin type A, as well as some other, more unorthodox treatments, which he was unwilling to discuss with me.

Margo was referred to me because of what Dr. West described as "unique and unusual activity that defies explanation".

Margo was only my patient for a little over three months, and then was out of my care for another four months or so before the strange incident that took her life, but during the time she was in my care, I saw much to corroborate that assessment, and very little that provided any answers, only more questions.

On our first few visits, she was quiet and withdrawn, not wanting to speak to me at all. I could tell by the way she held herself, and by the way she squinted and winced that she was in pain. I offered to dim the lights and she thanked me.

"How long have you had the headaches?" I asked her, and she waved her hand in the air as if to say *forever.*

"But not like this," I ventured, and she hesitantly shook her head.

Margo was recently married. I asked her how she was enjoying married life, how her husband dealt with her headaches.

"He's wonderful," she said, smiling gratefully. "He urged me to go to the study, and further, to come and see you. He's concerned."

"Of course," I said.

"His family is very religious," she added. "His grandmother wanted to call in an exorcist. She thinks I'm being demonically oppressed."

"What do you make of that?" I asked her, trying not to show any bias.

She stared at me and didn't say anything one way or the other.

"Do you mind if I smoke?" she asked instead.

I nodded, and found an ashtray for her.

"I don't even like it," she said, staring at the lit cigarette in her hand, trailing a plume of smoke. "But ever since the study, I crave it. Doctor West, he gave us

("There are lines scratched out," I told Penny. "Maybe Dr. Howard reconsidered including this passage in his journal."

"Probably protecting this colleague of his," Penny suggested. "This Dr. West. What was done to this woman?")

On our third visit, Margo finally showed some willingness to talk about her other symptoms. She showed up looking weak and ragged, with obvious signs of both mental and physical fatigue. She admitted that she wasn't sleeping, and I asked if she had any ideas why that might be.

She smiled weakly and said that she had an overactive imagination – that her mind raced, and that she couldn't turn her brain off.

"What do you think about?" I asked her. "Is it worries, or perhaps planning for the next day's activities? It's not uncommon for..."

"No, it's not that at all," she said, and then she told me about her inner voice. "I hear a voice. It speaks to me. It... *tells me things.*"

I was intrigued. I'd read about rare cases of schizophrenics with such symptoms – fully realized personalities that they hold conversations with. There were so many hoaxes, so many media-hungry frauds about, that I'd been terribly skeptical about ever encountering the real thing. I don't believe in the so-called Multiple Personality Disorder that has become fashionable in pop psychology circles. So I proceeded with caution. If this was merely an auditory hallucination or a delusion, there were pharmacological solutions that had proven quite successful in many cases.

"You think I'm crazy," she said, pulling her knees to her chest in a protective gesture.

"Not at all," I assured her. You're here to discover what's causing your distress. I'm willing to explore any and all avenues to help you with that quest."

She still looked skeptical. I feared losing her trust.

"I thought I saw a ghost once," I confided in her. "And I don't believe in ghosts. But to this day, I cannot rationally explain what it is I saw. And so I remain open to the possibility of the impossible. *There are more things in heaven and earth, Horatio, than are dreamt of in your philosophy.*"

"A man of science quoting Shakespeare?" she smirked, raising a curious eyebrow. Looking back, I'm quite sure that's the moment I fell in love with her.

March 15, 1974

I knew that I should have referred Margo to another doctor, but I was weak, and I was still very professionally curious about her condition. She confided that the voice was not audible ("How could it be?" she asked as if the answer was obvious. "My husband sleeps beside me and is never disturbed, while I lay awake all night with this chatter in my head") and that it was, in fact, the same voice every time. It wasn't erratic; in fact, it was calm, and friendly.

"It tells me stories," she said. "At first, they were sweet, but lately, they've begun to scare me."

"Why is that?" I asked.

"The stories are horrible," she said, looking pale. "They are the stuff of nightmares, only I can't wake up and chase them away by turning on the light."

"Do you remember any of them?" I asked.

"Every single one of them," she said, and began to tear up. "I can't forget them. I could recite them to the letter, as if they were carved into my brain."

I suggested it might be therapeutic if she told me one of the stories, and I could tell she didn't want to. I sat myself down on the arm of the big chair she was in, and took her hand. Physical contact is not unknown in the practice of psychiatry, but I cannot lie and say that this was not the first step over the line. Once that first step was made, the next few were much quicker and easier.

"Would you like a drink?" I suggested. Her hand was trembling.

"Yes," she said without hesitation. "Yes please."

I've reproduced the story she told me here to the best I can recall. I have not the skill with words that she, or whoever – or *whatever* it was within her that told this tale had, but I will try to at least tell the main points of the story for your consideration. She called the tale *Paraxenogenesis*.

❧

"What?" Penny asked, taken aback. We had situated ourselves on the sofa and were reading through the account, trying to understand what this journal might have to do with our missing Jessica. Here we'd found what seemed like the first connection.

"That's the name of one of her stories," I said. "I recognize it, too."

"Well, read the story," Penny urged. "Is it the same?"

"That's kind of a distinct name for it to be a coincidence, don't you think?"

Penny shrugged. "What's it even mean?"

"If I remember correctly from Jessica's story, it means *strange birth*," I explained, and turned my attention back to the book. Several pages were torn out.

"It's gone," Penny stated the obvious. "That's kind of convenient, don't you think?"

"Quite the opposite, I'd say. But still," I said, "I'd bet the farm those pages contained Jessica's story."

"You don't own a farm," Penny mumbled.

"You know what I mean."

"So, what?" she asked. "You figure this *Margo* is actually Jessica?"

"No," I said. "This Dr. Howard person said that Margo is dead."

Penny sighed and motioned for me to keep reading.

March 17, 1974

Margo began to refer to the voice in her head as *he*. At first it was a non-specific *it*, but now that she is more comfortable with me, she confessed to me that it was a man's voice. She told me, after we'd finished making love, that it wasn't anyone she recognized. We'd spoken of various theories – that perhaps it was a voice from her past, surfacing through her self-conscious. That the creativity was hers, but that maybe, for some reason, she'd erected a mental block that didn't allow her to accept her own brilliant imagination. But the more she spoke about the voice, the more it seemed like this voice was not just echoes, but was somehow – and I hesitate to use this word, because I cannot explain it – *independent*.

I suggested hypnosis to her, and she was amenable to the idea. I wish I'd never brought it up, but what's done cannot be undone.

I recorded the session, and I don't know how to interpret the results, and so I won't try. I have merely included the transcription here, with the best description I could. Make of it what you will.

Taped to the bottom of the page was a well-preserved envelope. It looked like it had been recently re-sealed.

"What is it?" Penny asked as I pulled it off the page and shook it.

"I think I know," I said, opening the envelope to confirm. Inside was a cassette tape with the word MARGO written on it.

"I feel like Alice," Penny said, eyes wide with curiosity.

"All that's missing are the words PLAY ME," I said, and went to dig up an old tape player.

KH: *Margo, can you hear me?*

M: *Yes.*

KH: *I want you to focus on me and me alone, Margo. Ignore everything but my voice, do you understand?*

M: *Yes, I understand.*

KH: *Tell me about the voice, Margo. When did you first hear the voice?*

M: *Always. Always in my dreams.*

KH: *Do you hear the voice every day?*

M: *Yes. He tells me bedtime stories. I used to like them. He told me I was special. I don't like them anymore. They scare me. He scares me.*

KH: *Margo, listen to me. The voice isn't a real person. It's just in your mind.*

(At this point, a strange noise appears on the tape that was not audible during the session. It sounds like the scratch of a needle across a record, and lasts about 25 seconds.)

M: *He says he loves me. He...*

KH: *Does he have a name, Margo? Does he ever tell you anything about himself?*

(Margo starts whimpering and makes a low, frightened sound.)

M: *(unintelligible)*

KH: *Margo?*

M: *(whispers) He's here.*

KH: *Who's here?*

M: *(screams) He's here!*

(More strange noises that I didn't hear during the session. What sounds like the growl of an animal, followed by what I imagine to be breaking glass. All of this is impossible, of course. I cannot account for what I am hearing.)

KH: *Margo, I want you to listen to me. Listen to the sound of my...*

M: *Fucking witch doctor bullshit charlatan prick!*

(Here I stood up abruptly, and knocked the tape recorder off the table. Among the commotion of me fumbling over myself, you can clearly hear horrible, guttural laughter. That voice – the same voice that had just spoken through Margo's mouth – continued laughing. I have it on tape. The voice – it's like nothing I've ever heard. I won't speculate on things that are impossible.)

KH: *Who are you?*

(More laughter. I should not have addressed Margo as if she were someone – something else. But even I got caught up in the moment.)

M: *She is mine, false doctor. Keep your filthy flesh off of my pet.*

(Here I feared the worst – that this manifestation was caused by guilt. That I had violated the doctor/patient relationship, and caused her to be unfaithful to her husband, who she still spoke of as sweet and supportive and understanding.)

KH: *Margo, I'm sorry. What I did was wrong, and I owe you my apology.*

M: *She is mine, witch doctor. She is*

(Here the tape squealed again – that same scratching noise, leading to a high-pitched scream of feedback. Again, I did not hear this during our session, but it corresponded to Margo's own scream, which ended the session.)

End of Transcript

Margo had no memory of anything that happened during the session, and I debated for days whether or not to play the tape for her. By the time I'd made the decision to play it for her, however, her mental state had changed, and in the end I decided against it.

March 18, 1974

I was in no way prepared for what Margo told me the next time I saw her after the session. I had given her some sedatives, and told her to try to get some sleep. I had hoped that the drugs would give her quiet, dreamless sleep, with no voices.

"I'm afraid," she told me. "He hates you so much, Kenneth. He screamed about you all night long, telling me all the horrible things he wants to do to you. And to the baby."

There's no easy way to find out that you are going to be the father of a child with another man's wife. I doubt there is a precedent for finding out that there is something – some presence, some being, some *creature* inhabiting that woman – and that it wants to kill you and your unborn child.

"I haven't been with T_____ in months," she promised. "The baby. It's yours."

I didn't argue with her. But I was suddenly as terrified as she was, as if her fear were somehow contagious. I had heard the voice of whatever it was that was inside of her. My scientific mind refused to believe that there was actually a separate being within this woman. The alternative, that somehow this voice – this personality – was some type of schism in Margo's mind, frightened me even more. I don't believe in ghosts or demons or monsters. But the mind is a mysterious thing, and I have sought my whole life to understand it. I did believe, at the time, that perhaps the real monster was Margo herself. And she stood in my office and told me that the monster wanted to kill me. I have since had my disbelief in impossible things challenged, and I do not know what to make of this new knowledge. I only know that it terrifies me. I do not believe in demons, but I am afraid of them.

After that session, I changed my locks. A couple of days later, I called Margo and suggested that perhaps we needed to stop seeing each other, even as doctor and patient. I offered to pay for an abortion, if that's what she wanted. I didn't hear back from her for two weeks. Then I got a phone message from her husband, telling me she'd suddenly become very ill, and had been asking for me. She wouldn't say why, but the headaches had gotten so bad that she was delirious with pain. He told me she was slurring her words and having trouble with balance, and had fallen more than once.

I was a coward, and didn't call him back. When he left a second message two days later, I returned his call and lied, telling him I was out of the country, and that I wouldn't be back for a month. I apologized that I wasn't able to be there for him and Margo, and I think I even sounded sincere.

I tried to convince myself that that was the last I would hear from them. It was ridiculous, of course. Margo was still unwell, and there was the small matter of the pregnancy, unless of course she decided to terminate. Though she had never asked me for the money, if that was the case.

Three months later, having not heard from Margo or her husband, I began to relax. I had moved on. I hadn't even listened to the tape of the hypnosis session in at least a month. Then I got a call from the hospital. Margo had been brought into the emergency room, unconscious and unresponsive. Her breathing was shallow, but her heart rate was elevated. According to her husband, she had been lying in bed for weeks, complaining as usual of a terrible headache, but she'd been getting progressively worse, and her head had begun to swell inexplicably. By the time I got there, Margo was convulsing, her head swollen so drastically that the skin was splitting. She was frothing at the mouth and unable to speak.

What happened next is impossible, of course, and unbelievable, but I swear it is true. I would not be leaving my home, my practice, and everyone I know, were it not so. I promised, under threat of death, to keep secret the things that I have seen, and this journal is nothing more than insurance. If something should happen to me – if they should break their word and some harm befalls me – then perhaps this journal will be my vindication.

I brought Margo into the diagnostics and imaging room, meaning to take a CT scan. Her head was swollen to the point where her facial features were nearly unrecognizable. I'd never seen anything like it. It was as if her head were being inflated like a beach ball.

There was just the three of us in the room – Margo and myself, and the X-ray technician, a young woman who would end her life wrapped around a telephone pole, accompanied by a writer from the National Enquirer. It was ruled an accident, of course, but I knew the moment I read the story who was responsible.

I laid Margo down on the table and began positioning her for the scan. It quickly became evident that she was not going to lie still without sedation. I held her hand, which was flexing involuntarily. I'm confident that she had no idea where she was, or that I was there. I cannot say with any certainty that she wasn't in pain anymore, despite the fact that she wasn't exhibiting any signs of awareness.

"Please," I asked the technician, whose name I will leave out of this record, "bring me..."

I was about to order a sedative, when Margo began convulsing, her body thrashing on the table so violently that the technician ran to assist me in trying to hold her still, for fear she would toss herself right off the table.

At this point, I would like to remind you that when last I had seen Margo, she had told me that she was pregnant. Five months later, I held her down on the examination table, and it would be my professional opinion that the woman who tossed and twisted in front of me was not pregnant. Whether she miscarried or aborted, I had no knowledge, but certainly if she were still pregnant, she would be showing, and Margo was thin and nearly emaciated. Seeing her body wasted away riddled me with guilt at having abandoned her.

"Doctor," the technician cried, dropping Margo's hand and backing away from the table. "What's wrong with her eyes?"

Margo's eyes had popped open, and were completely red. A thick film of blood pooled over them, obscuring both the white and the iris, and trickling down her cheeks.

Something... *moved* behind her skin. I watched in disbelief and horror as her face contorted, her mouth opening wide and her jaw distending.

"Her face," I said, stunned. "What's happening to her face?"

Margo screamed, and her back arched up off the table, her hands clawing at the air for something to hold on to, and finding my shirt, gripping it so tightly that it tore. The air was suddenly filled with the smell of blood and something else – something that smelled like rotting garbage, or a dead animal.

"Her face," I repeated, watching in disbelief as the skin of Margo's face stretched outward, her face taking on grotesque, unnatural shapes, as if something were inside her, pushing its way out.

Then her skin burst, and her scream was abruptly cut short. Another scream filled the air, this time from the technician, who had braced herself against a wall in horror.

Margo's body fell lifeless to the table, but the skin of her face still moved. I was frozen with fear, and could only watch as something, some pale thing crawled its way out from inside the dead woman's head, half-formed but humanoid. The screaming stopped, and there was an unsettling silence in the room, as we watched this thing, covered in a mixture of blood and some sort of black, viscous slime, emerge onto the examination table, trailing behind it what I can only describe as a sort of umbilical cord, the other end of which seemed to be attached to Margo's spinal column. In the brief moments I had to examine the body, I discovered that Margo's brain was completely missing, and we could not even begin to try to answer even the simplest of the questions that was plaguing us, namely, how was she even alive?

The child (for that's what I've come to think of it as) was female, and in my opinion, human – for what else could she be? I didn't have more than a few moments, once my shock passed, to look over her. No sooner had I cut the umbilical cord and tied off the end, than the doors of the examination room burst open and three women walked in and closed the door behind them. While two of them stood guard, the third approached me with arms held out, a look of what I can now describe as religious fervour in her face.

"The child!" she exclaimed. "It's true."

"Who are you?" I asked. "What do you know about this?"

"We heard the cries all night," she said. "We followed the sound of the beast. We call him the Raconteur, and you hold his child in your arms. You do not know how blessed you are to have borne witness to this."

Suddenly I felt terribly protective of the child. I didn't know anything about any beast or Raconteur but a strange paternal instinct came over me and I knew I couldn't let these women (whoever they were) take her.

The child in my arms began to wail, and I looked into her face – her strangely frightening face, with its skin turning purple with rage.

"Please," the woman held out her arms to take the baby from me, and I hesitated.

"Who are you?" I asked, reluctant to hand her the child.

"You have no idea what you have in your arms," she said. "Give her to me. I will keep her safe. I will help her become what the prophecies say."

"And what is that?"

"The words made flesh," she said, and despite my disbelief, I was filled with what I can only imagine was a sort of religious terror. "The walking, breathing personification of the stories."

I handed her the baby, and she quickly turned away as if to leave. I reached out to stop her, but was suddenly restrained by the other two women, who stepped forward and grabbed both of my arms, allowing the third woman to escape with the child. The technician had collapsed on the floor, and was sitting with her head in her hands, crying and moaning.

They stayed long enough to issue threats and promises, and to advise us not to find them, or the child. Then they moved Margo's body back onto the gurney we had brought her in on, covered it up with a sheet, and rolled it out the door.

I never saw any of them ever again. I've kept quiet about everything that I've seen and heard. I didn't even say anything to the police when they came by to question me about Margo's death. Hers and her husband's, actually. Their bodies had been found in their home, an apparent murder/suicide. The story seemed to be that T_____ had shot his wife in the face with a 12-gauge shotgun, and then turned the gun on himself.

I told the police that they had a troubled marriage, and that while Margo had never specifically confessed to it, that I suspected abuse. I acted suitably shocked and upset at the loss, and nothing more was ever said on the matter.

Five days ago, I saw the news article about a car crash. The bodies were identified as that of the technician who had been with me that day, and a woman who was well known as a writer for several tabloid magazines, most recently, the National Enquirer.

I knew that it was time for me to move on. I am giving up my private practice. I've been in touch with an old friend, who's invited me to come and work with him at a new mental hospital upstate. It's been so long since I've done hands-on clinical work, but I am anxious to relocate and start anew. The work promises to be rewarding, and will give me an opportunity to study abnormal psychology on a daily basis. I've had so many of my pre-conceived notions and beliefs challenged, and I can no longer continue to call things impossible. I am ready to believe anything, no matter how strange.

I closed the book. That was the last of it. The next few pages were torn out.

"It's bullshit," Penny said, but her protest was unconvincing. "That's like something out of one of her damned stories."

I didn't say anything. The journal could be the ravings of a lunatic, or just creative writing. But there were news clippings attached of the murder/suicide of a couple, just as Dr. Howard described. The names were blacked out, but I could put two and two together. There was another clipping that corresponded to the death of the technician and the reporter, names also removed.

Poughkeepsie Journal, December 27, 1973

Husband and Wife Dead in Apparent Murder-Suicide

T████ and M█████ E███ were discovered early yesterday morning in their Poughkeepsie home, both with fatal gunshot wounds to the head. Friends of the family say that Mrs. E███ had suffered a long illness and had been bed-ridden for several months after a tragic miscarriage. Police say that there was a history of violence in the E███ household, with several domestic disturbance calls in the past year.

"The holidays can be really hard on some people," Sheriff Wallace remarked. "It's a terrible thing. Thank God there were no kids involved."

Poughkeepsie Journal, March 12, 1974

Ice Storm Claims Two in Tragic Accident

Local writer, J█ E███, 33, and E██ K████, 45, were found dead at the scene last night at the intersection of Montgomery and Jefferson, just north of Eastman Park. They were involved in a collision with a Brinks truck, driven by Richard Prendergast. Mr. Prendergast was questioned by the police at the scene, and testified that the car driven by Mrs. K███ was moving exceptionally fast, and as he approached from the south toward the intersection, he didn't see the car coming until it was too late. Mrs. K███'s car either ran the stop sign, or perhaps was unable to stop due to recent icy conditions. No charges have been made against Mr. Prendergast. Miss E███ was a local celebrity of sorts, being well known for her Strange Tales column in the National Enquirer. Mrs. K███ was a veteran nurse at St. Francis Hospital.

The next date in the book was nearly thirty years later.

August 20, 2001

I think I've found her. After all these years of keeping my eyes and ears open for stories of the unusual – no matter how strange or unbelievable – I believe that she may have actually come back to me. Whether she is aware of my existence, or whether this is just a coincidence, I don't know, and that uncertainty frightens me.

I have been at Arcadia Heights now for almost thirty years, and I have seen a great many things that have baffled and confounded me. There have been cases of what some might have called multiple personality disorder but were, in fact, elaborate frauds, sometimes carried out by the patient, and sometimes, it's sad to say, carried out by psychiatrists in collusion with their vulnerable patients. These were the most despicable – media friendly narcissists looking to make a name for themselves with high profile, controversial cases.

Then there was Mary. Mary claimed to have met the devil once, and said that the devil had come back to her – that the devil was now a patient at Arcadia Heights.

When Mary came to us, she could hardly speak at all – her mouth was severely disfigured. She'd done it to herself, she wrote, so that she couldn't speak of what she knew. Of course, we asked her what exactly it was that was so horrible she couldn't talk about it, but she refused. Since she's been here, her verbal skills have improved immensely, but if she really has something to say, she prefers to write it. She's quite gifted, actually, and we encourage her to write out her thoughts. It seems to be therapeutic.

Mary had become withdrawn and agitated, refusing to eat or take her medication. There was an incident, in which one of our patients was terribly burned. It was ruled an accident – somehow, the patient had gotten some matches from lock up, and was playing with them and accidentally set fire to herself. Many of the patients were understandably upset, but none more so than Mary. Mary insisted that the devil had done it. She said that Rebecca had stolen the devil's cigarettes, and so the devil had set fire to her as payback. I asked Mary to tell me about the devil, and this is what she wrote.

Mary S. August 2, 2001

I knew it from the moment she arrived. The second she looked at me across the lounge, I saw the black in her eyes and I knew it was her.

"Quiet, Mary," was all Nurse Hadlam said when I told her. "Don't worry about her. She won't be here long. Look, your show is on."

But I couldn't enjoy it, couldn't solve the puzzles and shout at the contestants with her in the room. It was like someone had wheeled in a block of ice and set it right behind me.

I've known the silent types before. They pass through, sometimes. Often they start talking again and get let go. Most of the time they don't bother me.

But some do. They stay silent not because they can't speak. They stay silent because they won't speak. They have nothing to say that anyone else will understand and they know it. They look at you and there's black in their eyes that goes right through their skulls and it would suck you in and chew you up if you let it.

I won't let it.

I couldn't sleep that night. Normally the evening pills send me off in twenty minutes but not this time. I knew she would be in the dorm next door – they had a free bed since Rebecca had been sent on to a secure unit. Sue from that dorm said they'd scrubbed off most of the scorch marks and I saw them bring in another bed from storage.

That's where she'd be, all right.

I tried to tell Nurse Hadlam they should put her in an isolation room, but she just told me to play my chess and leave it be. I knew I shouldn't have bothered. They never do what I tell them, even when I'm right, which I am. Sometimes.

I suck on my teeth. Count them with my tongue. That sometimes distracts me. Count the teeth, skip the gaps, and then count the rest.

Not tonight.

I stare over the gently breathing forms of Annie and Biting Lil to my own dorm door. I swear I can almost see her standing beyond the glass. But I blink and she's gone.

I usually know when what I'm seeing is real or not. This time I couldn't tell.

I blame myself for what happened to Mary. I should have taken her seriously. But when I read her case file, I wrote her off as paranoid and delusional. She wasn't just hearing voices or lying compulsively about little things – she'd claimed to have met the devil. Reading her initial story – the one she'd written us upon intake, once her mental state had improved enough for her to be mostly coherent, I dismissed her. Her story was too incredible, and I didn't want to believe it.

Mary S_____, 38 years old, unmarried. Former truck driver. Brought to emergency unit March 12, 1998, suffering self-inflicted wounds to mouth and face. Displays persistent symptoms of paranoia and disorganized thinking, including a constant insistence that she has met the devil, and that he spoke to her in the language of the angels and demons. She alternates between fear and an elevated sense of self. She claims to have secrets that she dare not tell anyone. Attached below is Mary's own self-report on the events of the night of March 12th.

Mary S. April 9, 1998

I was sitting at a truck stop diner in the middle of nowhere, in one of those states that all look the same once you've driven through them enough times when she sat down. Normally, it's my policy not to talk to strangers – or anyone for that matter – at this kind of place. There are dives and then there are dives, if you know what I mean. But I stared at her a minute too long and before I knew it, she'd slid into the booth across from me. I can't tell you what drew my eye – can't tell you what she was wearing or even what she looked like, she sat across from me for all of an hour – but I think it was her eyes. Not the color – they could have been brown or blue or neon-fucking-purple – but they had this look, like she'd stared into the pit of hell itself and not only survived it, but gave it the middle finger and a laugh and said all seven circles better damn well prepare themselves.

I was halfway through my pie – apple that tasted like it'd been sitting under a heat lamp for longer than I'd been alive – when she plopped herself on the cracking plastic bench and leaned her elbows on the table and asked me about rats.

"Rats?" I put down my fork and fought the urge to look around. I have a phobia of the bastards, to be honest, but I didn't want to tell her that. "What about rats?"

"They say when it comes – the Big One, The End of All Things, the Apocalypse – that only the rats and cockroaches will survive," she said. "You know why?"

"Uhhh…" I looked around, wondering if I was in some sort of hallucination brought on by food poisoning from the pie or if I'd fallen asleep after a long day of driving.

"They know something most people don't – they know that to survive, sometimes you've got to play dirty. Vermin aren't afraid of a little muck." She reached across and picked up a piece of apple and popped it in her mouth, sucking it down with a relish and licking her fingers in a way that made me wonder if this was some sort of come on.

"People are stupid," she said, drilling me with that gaze of hers.

I said I'd seen plenty to prove her right and asked what her point was. She ignored my question and asked if I wanted to know what made people stupid. At this point, I was thinking she was on some kind of bender and maybe it was best to just humor her until she decided to go harass someone else. So I said no and why didn't she enlighten me.

"Because they're afraid of things like spiders and roaches and…" she looked me over appraisingly, "rats. There are worse things to fear than rodents and things that go bump in the night. Things that go bump are stupid. The smart ones know that darkness is no good if you make enough noise to wake the dead."

"So what should we be afraid of, then?" I asked in spite of myself.

She smiled – reminding me of a cat sizing up dinner, which would make me the rat, I suppose – and asked if I'd seen things I couldn't explain. I shrugged and said who hasn't? But I felt a chill run up my spine. If you drive for long enough and late enough, running on two hours of sleep in four days, you start to question your sanity. I couldn't un-see half the things I wanted to, and I didn't want to see half the things I'd heard about. She reached for another bite of my pie without taking her eyes off me.

"I was like any other wide-eyed seventeen year old – working a dead-beat job in a place like this." She jerked her head towards the counter. "It was like any other roadside cafe in any other roadside town. Nowhere, U.S.A. Population: An ever-rotating crew of drunks, perverts, and dried-up dreamers. I spent my days smelling like sweat and grease and the breath of a dozen truckers sucking in the already stale air at the diner and breathing it back out through their rotting pie-holes and my nights sleeping with a plastic bag of money under my pillow."

She said she was working double shifts and ferreting away every last dime she earned in tips, but it wasn't enough, and after months of eating Ramen two meals a day and sending out the stories she was writing and getting enough rejection letters to paper the walls of her motel room twice over, she decided she'd had enough. It was dark and windy and she hadn't been able to afford her nightly bowl of lukewarm Ramen, so the bottle of Evan Williams she got from the gas station down the street went quicker than it might have on a full stomach. She started walking down the side of the highway, part of her wanted to hitch a ride – try another town on another dark road – and part of her wanted to lie down on the dotted line until something came to sign her off into oblivion. It was well into the dead of night and no headlights flashed across the horizon. There was nothing to break that inky blackness between midnight and dawn and she found herself humming as she walked. It was an old blues song the cook at the diner had taught her, about a singer down on his luck, looking for fame and fortune who finds himself at the crossroads, the legendary place between worlds where deals can be made. She didn't believe in God and she wasn't too sure about the Devil, though she'd seen more proof of his existence than the heavenly Wizard of Oz. The sky was starting to fade to purple with lighter gray rimming the horizon, like a bruise, when she found herself clawing a hole in the dirt. She could taste grit along with whiskey as she thrust her driver's license into the dirt at the center of two county roads and clumsily covered it up. The wind picked up, blowing the damp, ancient smell of swamps and muddy water across the sky. For a moment, she thought she felt the ground trembling before she realized she was shaking, a side effect of the chilly breeze and the Evan Williams. She started to laugh.

"Well, I'll be damned. Even the Devil doesn't want my soul."

"I wouldn't be so sure." The voice slid over her like silk on bare skin.

She turned and looked up at a tall, thin man. No horns, no pitchfork.

"Where's the golden fiddle?" she asked, hearing the slur in her words.

The man laughed, skin stretching tight against his skull. The wind whipped the tails of his expensive looking coat against his lanky legs as he bent over slightly, still chuckling.

"I go by many names, it's true," he said finally, wiping at his eyes. "But none of them is Lucifer. Your mother called me the Raconteur."

"My mother?"

But the man, or whatever he was, just smiled and shook a boney finger at her.

"Ne'er mind that for now. You called on me. Why?"

"Are you g'nna grant my wish?" she asked, scrambling unsteadily to her feet.

"Do I look like a genie or fairy godmother to you?" he asked. There was still amusement in the velvet voice, but it crackled like static, now.

"No. Look, I don't care if you're a demon or an angel or some voodoo spirit. You're here and I'm here, so let's not waste any more time." She told herself her knees were only shaking from the whiskey and the breeze that sent goosebumps across her bare arms.

"You want to be free of this place and you want to worm your way into the minds and the hearts of the grubby, squalling masses with the written word." His black eyes flicked over her like a whip, cleaving aside flesh, bone, and spirit.

"Yes." She almost gagged on the word.

"And I s'pose you're offering your soul?" His tone said she could have offered him the decaying corpse of an opossum and he'd be more willing to accept it.

She nodded, clutching the bottle of Evan Williams to her chest like a talisman.

The tall man tapped a finger on his thin lips, considering. A slow, reptilian smile creased his face and his eyes narrowed. "I'm afraid I'll have to refuse. But I've got something a little better in mind."

"...And that's how I became the host for a demon. For five years I shared the attic with that bastard." She tapped a finger against her temple. "I got out of that shithole town and started writing. I wrote until my fingers bled, until my skin flaked, until I couldn't tell my stomach from my spine. And then I kept writing."

"You said five years. What happened then?" I couldn't believe I was asking this question. I couldn't believe I was still sitting at the same table with an unhinged loony. I couldn't believe *her*. I couldn't.

She grinned at me and again, I was reminded of a predator regarding its helpless, squirming prey. But not a cat this time, more like a snake, ready to unhinge its jaw and swallow me whole.

"He couldn't take it. He said five years rooming with my soul was worse than having no body at all." She paused, reaching for another chunk of soggy apple, dripping in congealed, artificial syrup and placed it delicately on her tongue. "But I have his memories. His thoughts. Eons of hellish experiences that even the most depraved human couldn't imagine in his worst nightmares. Endless stories, countless ideas, all part of me. So much brilliant darkness and horror that sometimes it frightens even me." She smirked and winked at me. "All of that awful, oozing, tormented shit. It's mine."

I didn't have a response to that, but it didn't seem to bother her. She stood and dropped a handful of singles on the table. She leaned in, close enough that I could feel her breath on my ear. Her lips seared the skin as she kissed me on the cheek.

And then she whispered something in my ear, got up and walked out the door. I don't remember much after that.

When they found Mary, she was sitting in the corner of the diner, pulling out her own teeth. She had nearly severed her tongue with a butter knife, and it took three strong men to restrain her. She broke her own jaw in the process, and it would be wired shut for the next five months after surgery. She spent a great deal of that time writing, and up until recently, that was the only way she communicated with us. Over the past few months, I observed improvement in the return of her speech. It was difficult to understand at times, and she was quite self-conscious about it, but I thought the fact that she was trying was a good sign. Then Nurse Hadlam came to me with some concerns, and insisted I speak to Mary. As is my habit, I recorded the session. I've reproduced that conversation here.

Nurse Hadlam: I don't know what it is, Doctor.
Patient covers ears with hands, and closes eyes tight.
NH: See? She's all over the place. Off her food. Won't engage in group. I've never seen her like this.
Doctor Kenneth Howard: Mary? Mary, is there anything the matter? Are you feeling ill?

Patient seems to disassociate. Her eyes roll back in her head as she throws it from side to side and issues a strange chuckle, and then inhales deeply – a wet, sucking sound.

KH: Mary? Mary, where were you just now?

Mary: A hole opened up in the floor and sucked you all in. I thought it was funny. It took you all away, and I thought I was safe, but then you called my name and I had to come back. It's scary here.

KH: Mary, what's wrong? What's scary?

M: I already said what's wrong. I ain't saying it again.

KH: What's she talking about?

NH: The new resident, in G Ward. Bell. Jessica Bell. The one they're hoping to clear and release next week.

KH: What about her, Mary?

(Mary becomes agitated.)

M: She's black inside. You need to keep her away from us.

KH: Has Jessica hurt you in some way, Mary?

NH: (Whispering) They've barely been in the same room.

M: Don't talk like I'm not here. Just 'cause I see things that aren't there don't mean I can't hear things that are.

NH: She's not even dangerous, that one. She's a sweetheart, is Jessica. Her release is coming up...

KH: Mary, I'm asking you. Has this patient hurt you?

M: No. But she will.

End of transcript.

She told me plainly that she was worried that Jessica would hurt her, and it seems she was right. The night that Jessica disappeared, we found Mary collapsed in the garden. She'd mutilated herself again, this time managing to tear her tongue out completely, as well as ripping off part of one ear. We never found her tongue. I visited her in the hospital, sitting by her side until she woke up. She stared at me, not with the anger and hatred I expected, but with pity. I gave her a pencil and paper, and she wrote me a short note:

Not your fault. Can't beat the devil.

"Who's the devil, Mary?"

Jessica, she wrote.

"Jessica did this to you?" I asked.

She shook her head and wrote: *No. Did it to myself. Only way to beat her. Can't speak the words. But she is the words. She needs to be stopped. She knows all the stories. They live inside her.*

I shuddered, as if a cold wind had just blown up my spine.

She is the words made flesh.

The feeling of a thirty-year-old nightmare returning. Now I had a name. Jessica. Could it really be her?

"What happened, Mary? Will you tell me? Can you write it down?"

She nodded, and motioned for the pencil and pad.

Mary S. August 19, 2001

It was in the gardens she finally cornered me. We were in sight of the big windows. A couple of the nurses were smoking nearby. I knew there was no way she could touch me without someone seeing but I still felt my knees go all to jelly. My morning pills had filled my head with wool. I blinked to try and see her better as she sidled up to me, like she was taking some pleasure stroll down some breezy promenade, beau on her arm, wind in her hair.

The smile on her face was soft. The blackness in her eyes was hard.

"Are you afraid of me like they say?"

I felt a jolt in my belly. It was the first time I'd heard her voice since that night at the diner, and it sent every inch of me crawling. I almost threw up on her feet but managed to swallow it back down.

"No," I said.

"Liar," she said. Her smile widened. Her black gaze slid to the nurses. Hadlam was watching us keenly. Jessica waved and smiled. I breathed deep, the smell of the garden's pines and wet grass almost pinning me to reality. I tried to tell her to go away but my tongue was thick and my brain muzzy.

"You aren't really speaking," I slurred. "You don't speak. It's in my head."

I swayed where I stood and she copied me, smiling the whole time.

"You're the only one who knows." Her singsong voice swirled in my mind as I tried to figure out if her lips were really moving. "We're going to keep it that way. Understand?"

I couldn't speak even if I wanted to. She stood and swayed a moment longer even though I'd finally managed to stay still, hair swooshing about her face, covering first one eye then the other.

Then she twirled and sauntered away, though in my eyes her head twisted and her eyes stayed on me right until she was out of sight.

I don't know where Jessica is now, or if she really is that child grown up. I never thought I'd see her again. I don't know how I missed the signs that she was dangerous. In our sessions, she stared at me intently. She showed great signs of intelligence and imagination, but also a compulsion for lies. She would alternate between talkative moods, where she would speak almost constantly, sometimes even engaging in strange forms of glossolalia, and days where she would not speak at all. She would tell me all kinds of fantastic stories about herself, some completely outside the realm of possibility. I got the feeling that she was often testing me, telling me stories and trying to ascertain how far she could push me before I called her on them. Some of the stories she told me were horrible, and unbelievably violent and disturbing, and at the time I suspected she was embellishing the tales to garner some sort of sympathy or attention. Now I wonder.

I need to do more research. The files I have on her are incomplete. I have no real idea where she came from or where she has been. I have compiled a list of the most likely incidents involving her. Once I had a name, it was a little easier to eliminate the false trails and focus in on those that seemed to lead back to her.

"Oh, shit," Penny said, pointing to a newspaper clipping that had been pasted to the pages. "I think I remember this."

I looked at the date on the clipping, and shook my head.

"What do you mean, you remember it? You weren't even born," I said. "I remember hearing about it when I was in high school. All those bodies. It was all over the news for about a week."

"We were talking about terrorism and al-Qaeda and stuff, and my teacher brought up the Evergreen Academy," Penny explained. "She said it was some secret training academy operating right under the government's nose. Taking rich kids and brainwashing them to be sleeper agents or something."

"A decade before the World Trade Center bombing, people weren't even prepared to think about the implications of a possible terrorist cell right on American soil. To be honest, I'd forgotten all about this." I admitted.

"But what's any of this got to do with our Jessica?" Penny wondered.

"I thought you said this was all bullshit?" I asked.

"I don't know," Penny allowed. "I mean, all that shit about the devil and demon possession is just the ravings of the clearly insane. Are you really going to listen to the testimony of a couple of paranoid schizophrenics?"

"That's fair..." I agreed.

"And I'm convinced that this Kenneth Howard quack is crazy as a shithouse rat, and should be locked up with his patients in a room with no sharp angles. Clearly, the man has his own problems vis-à-vis paranoid delusions. But maybe, in his obsessive quest to find some bizarre story, he stumbled on to something."

Sacramento Bee, June 5, 1990

The Sacramento Bee

TUESDAY July 5th, 1990

UNSPEAKABLE HORRORS AT EVERGREEN ACADEMY

Sixty-Eight Bodies and Counting as Federal Agents Explore Grounds

Responding to an anonymous call, Sacramento Police arrived at Evergreen Academy, a prestigious preparatory school set on its own 100 acres outside of Rancho Cordova, to find the bodies of over fifty people, left for dead in what is being described as the aftermath of some sort of war games.

The FBI was immediately brought in, and while no names have been released yet, is has been confirmed that many, but not all, of the victims were students at the academy. Not a single living person was found on the grounds, and no arrests have yet been made. Startling discoveries were made, however, upon entry to the school itself. See photos and continued story, B13

Glickman Real Estate Collapse

UNSPEAKABLE HORRORS AT EVERGREEN ACADEMY
Sixty-Eight Bodies and Counting
as Federal Agents Explore Grounds

Responding to an anonymous call, Sacramento Police arrived at Evergreen Academy, a prestigious preparatory school set on its own 100 acres outside of Rancho Cordova, to find the bodies of over fifty people, left for dead in what is being described as the aftermath of some sort of war games.

The FBI was immediately brought in, and while no names have been released yet, is (sic) has been confirmed that many, but not all, of the victims were students at the academy. Not a single living person was found on the grounds, and no arrests have yet been made. Startling discoveries were made, however, upon entry to the school itself. See photos and continued story, B13

JESSICA

Excerpt from The Evergreen Kids by M. Haley, Copyright 1997, Harcourt Brace Jovanovich, New York.

I wasn't looking for Jessica. I'd heard a rumour that there was a survivor of the whole Evergreen affair, and I started asking around. I'd gotten a vague description – dark hair, pale skin. Something about an oddly shaped scar. And a name. Just one name – Jessica, no last name. She found me in a bar in Baltimore, and cornered me, started asking me a bunch of questions. It felt like she was quizzing me – no, it was more intrusive than that – it felt like she was dissecting me, and I guess she didn't find anything that scared her off, because she told me her name, and said that she heard I was looking for her.

I was sceptical. Anybody could have caught wind of the fact that I was digging into the Evergreen thing. Christ, it had been five years, and except for that initial write up, nobody had published anything. It felt wrong to me, like someone had swept it under the carpet. But with no witnesses, there was no story. So when Jessica told me that she had been there, I needed some convincing. I needed to hear more. Like who was she, and where did she come from, and how did she end up at Evergreen, and where had she been all this time?

We ordered a pitcher of beer, and Jessica told me a lot of stories. Some of them felt false and some of them felt true, but she told them all with such passion and sincerity you never knew which was which. I remember the way her eyes sparkled as she spoke in soft, dusky tones, and the way she used her hands to describe impossible-to-imagine things. She captivated me with every one of her stories. This story in particular, though, I believed. I have no idea where she is now, but wherever she is, I wonder if she still tells the tale of the Evergreen kids.

Jessica was sixteen. It was late, and she was asleep in bed. Strange noises bled into her dreams: the clicking of a barrel, the creak of a floorboard, someone clearing their throat... When she abruptly awoke, three armed three men in keffiyehs and camo gear were standing in the latest in a string of foster home bedrooms: one sitting on the beanbag in the corner, one placidly admiring the rock band poster on the wall, and one staring her down with sunglasses on, though it was long past midnight.

Jessica saw herself reflected in his Oakleys. She opened her mouth to shriek but he held one finger to his lips. He lifted the barrel and signalled for her to follow him, walking backwards into the hall. The other two grabbed her arms. They trundled downstairs, Jessica still in her favourite skull pyjamas.

Outside, a white van with *Evergreen* painted on the side was parked haphazardly on the lawn. Moonlight spilled upon a group of young people sitting in the rear. They were all in nightclothes, too. One girl clutched a teddy bear.

"What the fuck is going on?" asked Jessica.

"No talking," barked Oakley.

She was bundled inside with the others. The door slammed shut, and it was pitch black in the back of the van.

The engine roared, rubber squealed, the van rattled at high speed. The teens inside were tossed around for hours, flesh on flesh on flesh, like some sexless orgy. At first they laughed but they quickly grew tired and rolled around in silence, not even apologising when they were thrown into someone else's lap or chest. It smelled rank, like sleep and sweat and piss and halitosis.

Eventually, the van slowed. The door heaved open and everyone tumbled out, dizzy, falling onto their knees.

Jessica was in the middle of a barren wasteland, just outside a wall of thorns and corrugated tin lined with guards in uniform and snarling pit bulls. She followed the men in keffiyehs through the gated entrance.

Hundreds of people were standing idly in front of what looked like an old colonial ranch: a long, low, white building with ornate balconies and pillars, covered in creepers, moss and bird shit. The word *Evergreen* was carved above the entrance.

Another man in sunglasses (Ray Bans this time) stood at the top of the steps, signalling for quiet. He gave a long speech, none of which was important but for the last line. Their mission, said Ray Bans, was to survive the night.

That's when the girl with the teddy bear made a break for it, hurtling back towards the van.

Oakley shot her in the back.

She gave a little yelp, like a kitten whose tail has been trodden on, and crumpled. Blood pooled around her, soaking her white nightgown.

Jessica watched and waited, but the girl didn't get up again.

They were given guns and fatigues. They were driven out into the woods in overland vehicles and dropped off separately, with no other in sight. Jessica watched the tan-coloured Jeep drive away, until she could no longer hear its tracks.

She tried to work out how to fire the gun.

The trigger jammed, and when she fired at a tree the force of it threw her backwards, stumbling, firing a second bullet into the stars.

Gunfire sounded in the distance, shouting and screaming. People began running in all directions, firing blindly. Jessica concealed herself behind a tree, listening to her own ragged breathing.

"We have to work together!" someone shouted.

"No, only one of us can live!" screamed someone else.

Bang. Bang. Bang.

Jessica heard movement and fired warning shots into the darkness, but no one appeared.

During the long hours she made up stories in her head, pretending to be an assassin and a spy and a soldier. Or maybe she was just playing a game, and none of this was really real.

Slow, unsteady footsteps.

She whirled around, seeing three shadowy figures.

Jessica positioned the gun in hand, finger on the trigger.

"I don't want to ki—' she began, but they charged at her, growling.

Instinctively, she fired off a round. Her whole body shook. She swung the gun in an arc as she attempted to reclaim control of it.

Three now lay dead, sprawled around her in a kind of triptych. They wore ragged, deep green jumpsuits and their skin was flaying, decaying. They had long, sharp fingernails and their mouths were covered in blood.

Their jumpsuits were embroidered with the word *Evergreen*.

Shivering, Jessica fled.

The woods were scattered with bodies, horribly mauled and mutilated.

She walked gracefully through the carnage, overcome by a strong, carnal desire to survive this bloody mess.

She covered her face with mud and decorated her fatigues with twigs and leaves. She shat in a hole beneath a tree. She worked out which direction led back to the colonial building, and trudged determinedly towards it.

A mile or two on, and Jessica found a campfire burning.

A group of four Evergreen kids in overalls sat around it, their skin pale and patchy. They were unarmed, but their mouths were bloodied.

They saw her approach, but did nothing.

Jessica locked and reloaded.

"I don't want to kill you," she tried, again. "But I'm vermin now, and this is how vermin survives. Sometimes you have to play dirty."

"No, no, please *do* kill us," one of them said.

"What?"

"Please kill us," the boy repeated.

Jessica frowned and chewed her lip, shifting the gun's weight in her hands.

It had to be some kind of trick.

"Why?" she said.

"We just want to die," said one of the others.

"Kill us, or we'll live forever like this."

"Please let our suffering be over," said another.

"What happened to you?" she asked.

"You name it, they've tried it on us."

Evergreen had once been an institution for troubled teenagers, they explained, whose parents signed disclaimers permitting their temporary imprisonment in this 'pioneering behavioural institution'. They hoped that their children would be returned to them anew, but Evergreen was being used by the government for covert tests and training exercises.

The story that hit the papers focussed on the secret training exercises and the war games. But according to Jessica, the children were being experimented on. Cutting edge steroid cocktails, nerve blockers, brain implants, surgeries, and dangerous cross-species gene splicing that would make Dr. Moreau seem positively harmless. And then finally, there was something else – something terrifying – they called it simply The Formula, and it seemed to halt death itself – but at a terrible strain on the recipient.

"We're not alive, but we're not dead either."

"I can see that," Jessica said, lowering the weapon a little.

"They'll never let us free. They don't want the world to know about us."

"There is no way out for us but death. We long for it."

"Please kill us," they repeated.

They were begging, and Jessica pitied them.

"I... I need to think about it a while," she said. "I'm tired."

As distant gunfire crackled, she sat around the fire with the Evergreen kids. Flames cast shadows on their horrific, corpse-like faces.

The sky was lightening, turning colours.

Together, they talked of the world as they'd once imagined it: a perfect, safe, happy place. They talked of their rosy gilded childhoods, in which they'd never feared. They talked of noodles and cartoons and camping and school; they talked of parties and Christmases and driving along the highway at night. They talked of everything they remembered that had never really existed.

At the break of dawn, four sequential shots resounded, echoing through the silence of the forest.

Jessica walked slowly towards the building in the distance, and disappeared.

Lansing State Journal, January 17, 2005

Lansing State Journal

Monday, January 17, 2005

ANGEL OF DEATH VISITS SUBURBIA

Forty-Seven Dead in Unexplained Mass Suicide

Twenty households have been touched by horror in Lansing, as police responded to multiple reports of gunshots between the hours of six and seven a.m. yesterday morning on Carson St., a normally quiet community in the Northwestside. Police arrived on the scene and were unable to get any response after knocking on several doors. They first entered the home of Steve and Angela Warburton, and found them both deceased, with evidence of gunshots being fired.

"We began canvassing the neighborhood," Sgt. Peterson reported. "We were hoping someone could tell us something about the Warburtons, but when we started knocking on doors, it quickly became apparent that something was terribly wrong."

All the deaths have been ruled, thus far, as suicides, but no further information has been released that would explain this strange occurrence, nor shed any light on what connection, other than the obvious, that the victims had with one another.

Two survivors were found, one a seemingly failed suicide was rushed to Sparrow Hospital and is listed in critical condition. The other, Alice Shelley, was found locked in her house, a seeming paranoid that had painted her windows black and had to be removed by force. The police would not comment if this Miss Shelley was somehow implicated in the events of January 16th, nor would they confirm rumors that she had been taken into Psychiatric care. *Continued on E7*

ANGEL OF DEATH VISITS SUBURBIA
Forty-Seven Dead in Unexplained Mass Suicide

Twenty households have been touched by horror in Lansing, as police responded to multiple reports of gunshots between the hours of six and seven a.m. yesterday morning on Carson St., a normally quiet community in the Northwestside. Police arrived on the scene and were unable to get any response after knocking on several doors. They first entered the home of Steve and Angela Warburton, and found them both deceased, with evidence of gunshots being fired.

"We began canvassing the neighborhood," Sgt. Peterson reported. "We were hoping someone could tell us something about the Warburtons, but when we started knocking on doors, it quickly became apparent that something was terribly wrong."

All the deaths have been ruled, thus far, as suicides, but no further information has been released that would explain this strange occurrence, nor shed any light on what connection, other than the obvious, that the victims had with one another.

Two survivors were found, one a seemingly failed suicide was rushed to Sparrow Hospital and is listed in critical condition. The other, Alice Shelley, was found locked in her house, a seeming paranoid that had painted her windows black and had to be removed by force. The police would not comment if this Miss Shelley was somehow implicated in the events of January 16th, nor would they confirm rumors that she had been taken into Psychiatric care.

Police transcript. Statement of A. Shelley, 42, Lansing, Michigan. Discovered in her home morning of January 16th, 2005. One of only two confirmed survivors.

When everything is in the shadows, then nothing is scary.

I used to take walks in the evening. Especially in the Fall. I loved the Fall. Night fell earlier and the air was cool. Fall was best for walking.

I lived in the neighborhood then. The sidewalks were old but well maintained. Walking through the neighborhood in the fall was the best. More curtains were opened. I knew I would see anything from a family sitting down to dinner, to kids doing their homework, to tired looking men watching football. Or shows about football. Or the news when they talked about football.

It was on these walks that I noticed something about houses that were lit up against the dark. The windows looked like eyes. Once I saw the windows as eyes, I couldn't see them any other way. Sometimes the curtains made them look like heavy lidded eyes or eyes lowered in suspicion. Sometimes they were hollow and sometimes they looked alien. But always like eyes. Except for her house. The windows at her house just looked like windows.

I don't remember when exactly she moved into the neighbourhood. They tell me her name was Jessica, but I never spoke to her. I only ever saw her – or I thought I did – once, staring out her window at me. After that day, I avoided that house altogether. Something about the way she stared at me chilled me to the bone. Something about her eyes...

The more I thought about the eyes (windows, dammit, I mean windows) the more I saw them everywhere. And forever after that day, all the eyes were *her* eyes. I saw them in department store doors and the freezers where they stored frozen pizza at the grocery. I saw them on buses and in puddles, on the chain link fence in front of the elementary school and in the window of the day old bread store. But mostly they were false. The only real eyes were in the houses where I walked.

After seeing the eyes, the walks continued but they were more hurried. No more strolling along taking long looks at the dinner scenes, watching candles get lit and drinks get spilled. No more watching kids yawn and rub their eyes and stick their tongue at the parent's backs for making them do their homework. I still looked in their windows, but I was only stealing glances. I had to look; I had to make sure the eyes weren't changing.

Night began coming sooner and the air went from crisp to cold and from cold to dangerous. I couldn't give up my walks, though. Something was wrong. I couldn't put my finger on what it was, exactly, but something wasn't quite right. I put plastic bags over my feet before putting on my snow boots. I covered my cheeks in petroleum jelly before wrapping a scarf around my head and walking my neighborhood. It took anywhere from twenty-seven to forty-three minutes to walk the neighborhood. It depended on how many neighbors were out and how many of them felt compelled to talk about the weather or complain about tax levies. Lately, the walk didn't take over twenty-seven minutes. The rest of the neighbors were indoors, warding themselves against the cold.

They were locking themselves in.

I knew, though. I knew when they locked their doors that they weren't alone behind their own walls. Something was wrong in my neighborhood. It was like something was haunting it.

I started noticing the shadows toward the end of November. It was bitterly cold, but still, nowhere as bad as it was going to get. It wasn't until January when I realized that if I wasn't careful, if I didn't cover *everything* then I might end up losing it. My earlobes were thick and made wearing earrings uncomfortable but that didn't mean I wanted to lose them to frostbite. Sometimes you suffered for your beauty.

In November, I was only wearing a skullcap and a scarf. The parka and the facemask and petroleum jelly were still five weeks away.

It was late in November and I remembered how much I used to love looking into windows in the evening and how that seemed to have been years ago instead of months. I stopped strolling about a month ago, about the time I started smelling smoke from fireplaces and the trees were just becoming bare. For the first time since the trees lost all their leaves, I strolled instead of walked and for the first time in a month I stared into windows.

The first time I saw something spring from a shadow, it scared me so much that I fell on my ass. The second time scared me just as bad, but I was ready for it and didn't fall.

After that day in November, the walks weren't about watching the windows and how they looked like eyes. The walks were about catching the shadows moving. Catching them lurching and sometimes springing.

Every night was as terrifying as the last because the people in their houses couldn't see the moving shadows. I never saw a single person flinch. How could they not see them? I could though and every night I thought for sure I would see what was moving in the shadows. I would see an edge or flash and once I was sure I saw one of the windows wink like an eye. Every night I would go home and question what I had seen by the time I got my front door unlocked. By the time I climbed into bed, I convinced myself that it was nothing, and that maybe I wouldn't go on my walk the next night.

But I was lying. I knew I was lying.

Each darkened house was my reprieve. Walking past them kept me from running home, screaming. The darkened houses had no stray shadows to jump from. The darkened houses were all shadows. They felt like comfort. But somehow, one night, I found myself in front of *her* house again. There were lights on, of course, but there were no shadows. Impossible as that sounds, *there were no shadows!*

I ran all the way home and locked myself in. I crawled into bed and buried myself in the covers and prayed.

Winter droned on and Spring was still nothing more than a rumor the last time I walked for a very long time. It was at the end of my walk. More houses were darkened than lit. The shadows were still moving, but they were slowing down. More lurching, less springing.

When I got to my house, the first thing I noticed was that both the front lights were on. I hadn't left them on, I'm sure of it. I'm quite compulsive about that kind of thing. The second thing I noticed was that the windows looked like eyes. And there were shadows. There were shadows all over my house.

There were no more walks after that night. I didn't want to see what was lurking in the shadows anymore. I wanted to make sure it stayed in the other houses.

The only way to be safe was to make sure I lived completely in the shadows. Heavy drapes weren't enough. Foil in the windows could fall from the glass. I smashed all my light bulbs and sprayed all the windows with black poster paint. Everything was shadows and my windows were just windows.

When everything is in the shadows, then nothing is scary.

June 2, 2010

Despite Miss Shelley's insistence that there was a woman named Jessica living in the neighbourhood, I have yet to be able to find any confirmation. There was no one named Jessica among the victims. There are no houses belonging to anyone named Jessica in the neighbourhood, no pictures of her, not even a piece of mail with the name Jessica on it. The only other survivor of the event makes no sense at all.

Gail Sherman was found unconscious in her home the morning of January 16th, 2005, the victim of a self-inflicted gunshot wound to the head. Miss Sherman was rushed to Sparrow Hospital where she had surgery to remove a bullet from behind her eye. She has lost the use of her left eye, and has some mild brain damage due to blood loss and oxygen debt, but is otherwise physically recovering. I requested an interview with her when I caught wind of the story of the suicides, and the name Jessica coming up in the police investigation. I explained to the police that I believed that this might be the same Jessica who had escaped from my care in 2001, that she might be dangerous. I assured them that I had no interest in interfering with their investigation, but only in locating my patient, and preventing more harm. They consented, but warned me that they hadn't been able to get much in the way of coherent thoughts from her. I have to say I agree. I didn't learn much from Miss Sherman, though perhaps her delusion is, in itself, more of a story than she might have told had she been in full possession of her wits.

Patient interview with Gail Sherman, survivor of Lansing mass suicide.

Doctor Kenneth Howard: What can you tell me about this Jessica person? Did you know her?

Gail Sherman: I know the truth about Jessica. Hand on heart, I know. She doesn't actually exist.

KH: I don't understand.

GS: I'm not saying that she isn't real. What I'm saying is that you won't ever recognize her. She doesn't wander the streets wearing a hockey mask, she isn't horribly disfigured, there are no fangs dripping with blood. She doesn't even have a birthmark on her cheek. She travels the world, but you'll never find her name on a passenger manifest. She doesn't even have a passport.

KH: I'm not any of those things, and neither are you, and yet, we're real? Are we not?

GS: (sighs) How do I explain this so you'll actually get it? She is everywhere. She is nowhere. Yes, you might well turn your head to look for her, even stare at the girl sitting opposite you. You won't see her.

KH: So she's a ghost?

GS: No. Here's how it goes. Your alarm has wrenched you from the best sleep ever, you can't quite focus your eyes on the time, let alone remember what day it is and who you are, perhaps even where you are. It's that kind of morning. Or, it's a weekend, you're lazing around watching crappy TV just because you can, and you fall asleep. You wake up with a jump that makes your heart pound and you can't quite work out if you've slept the clock round to the next day, or if you've just nodded off for ten minutes. You're confused.

KH: Are you asking if I'm confused?

GS: No, I'm telling you — that's your state of mind. You're confused, so you tumble out of bed or off the sofa, stagger to the bathroom, turn on the light and blink — a lot. You decide you need to freshen up. You run the cold tap, suck at the blissfully cold jet of water and splash it on your face. You reach for the towel and dry yourself off, trying to wake up. You look up, peer at the mirror above the sink — and your heart does a sick somersault.

What the hell was that?

You screw your eyes shut and shake your head, trying to clear your mind and rid yourself of the horrific thing that you saw — for thing is the only way to describe it. If you had to write it down, you couldn't. If the police ever asked you to put together an e-fit, you couldn't. All you could say is that it was the most horrifying thing you have ever seen. It reminds you of rotting corpses bubbling to the surface of stinking swamps, a body farm, souls in abject torture, moist skin oozing with yellow-green-grey pustules, decaying flesh and the darkest of dark hearts.

This throws you off-kilter, but in the bright light of summer days bursting with promise and laughter, you forget. Life is too short, too hectic to hold on to horror. You're a busy girl about town. You're a go-getter. You're young, energetic, happy, fulfilled. You don't have time for flights of fancy and things half-seen, or not-quite-half-seen out of the corner of a bleary, sleep-encrusted eye.

You forget.

KH: Sounds like something best forgotten. We all have this sort of waking nightmares sometimes. The important thing is knowing the difference between what's real and what's not.

GS: Don't you wish you knew? Don't you wish could forget completely? But you can't. You remember. You have no choice. You know who you are. You're cruising around your shining glass-walled city. You're surrounded by skyscrapers and high-end stores with floor to ceiling windows filled with artful displays just begging you to fall in love with the latest handbags, shoes, jewelry and phones. You're a marketer's delight. You just can't help but look and drool and sigh over all the products you absolutely must possess to complete your lifestyle.

You simply can't resist giving your reflection the once-over with a critical eye. You look at your ghostly self and imagine wearing those perfect shoes with your hair just so, and you preen.

And then you don't. And then you're back in the bathroom with those blurry eyes and that until-now-forgotten memory.

KH: Do you have trouble concentrating, Gail? Do you ever lose track of time, maybe find yourself somewhere and you don't know how you got there?

GS: (She seems to be ignoring me, or perhaps not hearing me at all.) You've seen it again. Only this time, this time it's much worse. Now your nostrils are drenched in the stench of rot and decomposition. Despair and horror are etched into your once worry-free, smooth skin. You are dark, deformed, ugly, bestial, carnal, dirty and foul. You can see your rotting soul. You are sepulchral, leprous and suppurating.

You shake your head, flick your hair, and everything returns to normal. You look around, expecting the gates of hell to be yawning open before you, but all you see are sleek limousines, perfect window displays, sales assistants floating silently on the other side of soundproof glass and customers dripping with luxury. Nobody is pointing, mouths wrenched open with silent screams, nobody is running away, nobody has a gun aimed at you. It's a normal Saturday.

Except it's not.

KH: No, it's not. Gail, what can you tell me about that night? That Saturday night when your neighbors took their own lives?

GS: (Agitated) No, no no! This time, you can't shrug it off. The stench of decay invades your nostrils and wraps itself around your mind. To you, your hands are bony talons tipped with broken, cracked, dirt-encrusted nails. To you, your hair feels greasy and knotted. To you, your breasts hang concave and pendulous from your rib-strung chest. To you, your breath is foul and your teeth are yellowing and decayed. But nobody else can see it.

Your friends make excuses. Your social life dwindles. You're nervy, jumpy, you're paranoid. Even though you don't want to, you check your reflection in mirrors and windows. You want to catch her unawares.

KH: Who, Gail? Who do you see in the mirrors and windows? Jessica?

GS: Yes, her. Jessica. But she's clever and twisted. You go looking for her, and she's not there. Weeks and months pass and you're a recluse, buried in your apartment, mirrors covered and curtains closed against the light. You're festering. One day, seized by claustrophobia, you venture out — out into the blessed fresh air, out into the sunshine, out into the world. You can't let this rule your life. You can't disappear.

KH: But you did disappear, Gail. The police found you in your bedroom, and you'd nailed the windows shut and locked all the doors. You hadn't been outside in weeks.

GS: Outside! Ha! That's where she pounces. That's when a stranger sees the crazy in your eyes, the rotting excuse for a human being that you've become and calls the police, the medics, the people with the power to subdue.

That's when you know. That's when you lock yourself away to protect the world, because you know the truth.

KH: What truth, Gail?

GS: The truth, doctor, the truth! Jessica is you! I am Jessica, doctor! Lock me away before I kill again!

End of Transcript.

Neither of these women seems to have anything of use in finding Jessica. I haven't seen her for over ten years now – since that night she escaped from Arcadia Heights. I've been looking for her but I cannot find anything concrete. I checked our records again, and she was checked in under the name Jessica B. Bell. I've no idea what the middle initial stands for. I am beginning to doubt if I'll ever see her again.

"I thought you said you made that B. Bell stuff up?" Penny asked, and I shrugged.

"She must have told me," I said. "Or maybe it was written on one of her stories. I honestly can't remember."

"Well, what do you make of that story – the one about all the suicides?"

I shivered, and shifted uncomfortably on the couch.

"It's creepy," I said. "But I don't see what it has to do with Jessica – *our* Jessica, anyway. I mean it's not exactly an uncommon name. And like you said – this doctor seems to be jumping at shadows, trying to string together a narrative out of thin air, smashing them together even when it doesn't make any sense. But this..."

I unfolded a piece of newsprint, a little more than two years old.

"This I remember clearly. This was right before Jessica showed up on our doorstep."

Toronto Star, June 6, 2012

TORONTO STAR

Wednesday, June 6, 2012 · thestar.com · EVENING THUNDERSTORMS HIGH 28C WEATHER MAP ON S10

Double Homicide in Yorkdale Home

Andrej and Elizabeth Popović were found murdered in their Yorkdale home this morning in what police are calling a vicious, senseless crime. The Popovićs were involved in countless charities, but most specifically, Safe Haven, a project that targeted at risk street children.

"It's a terrible tragedy," a representative from Safe Haven told us. "The Popovićs were like guardian angels. Safe Haven isn't just a place to go to keep you away from the dealers and the pimps. They gave me a part-time job and are helping me take college courses. A year ago I was homeless and starving to death. Today, I'm working my way to a degree, and I'm helping other kids like me get off the streets. Whoever killed them is a monster. A real monster."

Police say they are looking for a recent lodger of the Popović's – the couple often took in troubled youth, helping them acclimate into the Safe Haven program. According to sources, the couple did have someone staying with them for the last few weeks before their murder, but no sign of anyone has been found.
Continued on A3

DOUBLE HOMICIDE IN YORKDALE HOME

Andrej and Elizabeth Popović were found murdered in their Yorkdale home this morning in what police are calling a vicious, senseless crime. The Popovićs were involved in countless charities, but most specifically, Safe Haven, a project that targeted at risk street children.

"It's a terrible tragedy," a representative from Safe Haven told us. "The Popovićs were like guardian angels. Safe Haven isn't just a place to go to keep you away from the dealers and the pimps. They gave me a part-time job and are helping me take college courses. A year ago I was homeless and starving to death. Today, I'm working my way to a degree, and I'm helping other kids like me get off the streets. Whoever killed them is a monster. A real monster."

Police say they are looking for a recent lodger of the Popovićs – the couple often took in troubled youth, helping them acclimate into the Safe Haven program. According to sources, the couple did have someone staying with them for the last few weeks before their murder, but no sign of anyone has been found.

JESSICA

June 19, 2012.

Two years, I've tried to put this whole thing out of my mind. Then tonight, out of the blue, a woman with news of Jessica visited me. I say visited, as if she came to the hospital and asked for me, or called up and introduced herself, maybe suggested we meet for coffee. What I should really say is that she accosted me. I was about to start my car when I suddenly felt cold steel against my neck, and a voice from the back seat tell me to keep calm, that she didn't want to hurt me. She tossed an envelope into the front seat.

"She said to give this to you. She said you'd know what to do with it."

"Who?" I asked, but she didn't answer. I caught a glimpse of her in my rear view mirror as she quickly got out of my car and ran off.

My heart pounded painfully in my chest, and my head spun. I'm getting too old for chasing ghosts.

I came home and locked myself in my office, hands trembling. If the woman in my car was who I thought she was, then I was closer than I'd ever been to finding Jessica again. After all, she had supposedly sat in the same room with her; spoken with her; listened to her stories.

I pulled out my copy of *The Evergreen Kids* and looked at the author photo.

I choked back tears. It was her. It was really her.

I stifled a little laugh, and thought that if I'd been carrying the book around, I could have gotten her autograph.

"Is that what I think it is?" Penny asked me, grabbing an envelope from out between the pages of the journal.

I nodded, and grabbed it back from her. It had a UK postmark on it, and was addressed to a woman named Elizabeth Popović, with a Toronto address. I read the news article again and there it was. One of the victims of a crime that had been all over the news a couple of years ago. A man and his wife, slain in their own home, the murderer never caught. But then there was something else about it that I couldn't remember. I'd been dealing with my own losses at the time, and didn't follow the news that closely. And then, of course, Jessica had shown up.

"Well, open it, already!" Penny commanded, and I complied. There were two different letters inside. The first was in Jessica's handwriting. I'd gotten used to deciphering it so that I could publish her stories. The second, I assumed was from the original sender.

Dear Doctor,

I understand you've been looking for me. I'm sure you've heard all kinds of stories, but you've truly got the wrong idea about me. I've been unfortunate enough to find myself in some strange situations, to be sure, but I promise you there's nothing sinister about me. Take this latest situation, for example. Poor Elizabeth didn't know who she was married to. This friend of hers was trying to warn her about me, when all the while Elizabeth was sleeping with the real monster. I found out more than I should have, and have gone into hiding. If the people who killed Andrej and Elizabeth knew I existed, I would not be long for this world. So I stole this letter – and anything else that might lead anyone to me, most of which I destroyed. But this letter I thought you might find interesting. The police are looking for answers, and they think that this mysterious lodger holds the key. I do, but not in the way they think, of course. You've been looking for answers about me – well, this is the only one I have to offer. I'll confess to one crime, though I really never did get to carry it out. When I found out who Andrej really was, I was planning on killing him myself. But it turns out he was hiding from people that were even worse than he was. Do yourself a favour and forget about me, Doctor. I think it would be safer for you.

To your health. Or, as they say in Serbia, *Za vaše zdravlje.*

Jessica

"Read it again," I said, passing the letter over. "Read it again, Penny, because I don't know what to make of it."

While Penny re-read Jessica's letter, I unfolded the second letter – heavy, expensive looking stationary, covered in elegant handwriting. Whoever this Andrea woman was, she had exquisite taste.

Elizabeth, my dear friend, I'm writing this to you with a heavy heart and a churning in the pit of my stomach which won't go away. Dark clouds have entered my mind, and I am caught entirely on the absolutely horrific story of a young girl, who may or may not be your very own mystery woman. I need you to find something out for me...

Let me start at the beginning. (I'd normally sing about it being a very good place to start, but what I'm about to disclose, and the potential ramifications... I don't think I could get a note out!) As part of my professional development, I'm required to attend various training days and seminars and, oh, you know the kind of thing. Anyway – part of the mandatory training is a day to cover Safeguarding Children, which is essentially a day of being exposed to some of the very worst things a human can inflict on one the youngest members of its species, with a view to making us all more vigilant workers in stopping it where we see it, and not being afraid to speak up, just in case we're on the money.

One of the case studies we had to look at detailed the rescue and subsequent fostering of a girl who grew up in an orphanage in Eastern Europe in the 1980s. I don't know if you know much of those places... I've seen documentaries, and whilst some are well-funded and well-run, the poorest and worst run institutions are nothing short of a life-sentence for the children who find themselves there. They all seem to be built of concrete, with broken windows and rooms full of abandoned children rocking back and forth in an effort to self-soothe.

Anyway, this particular institution had been ravaged by some kind of respiratory condition, and the children were dropping like flies, given they were all malnourished, unloved and too ill clothed to manage the winter temperatures. There were only a few staff members, all of whom were instructed flat-out to bury the dead before they infected the living, whilst trying to keep the remaining children alive. To little avail, sadly, but a few children were spared the disease by virtue of having recently had their tonsils removed (forcibly – tied to a chair, with no anaesthetic, because it cost too much) and were recuperating in a different part of the orphanage.

They tie them to their cots while they're recovering from surgery. Did you know that? They don't want them to be able to disturb the healing process, so they strap them down. Little kids who've just been subjected to incredible pain and violation (they take the tonsils out as a precaution, because they think that it will prevent them getting throat infections later, which would require expensive antibiotics – damn their ignorance and lack of funds!) – left for hours or days with their wrists butterflied against the railings, only given a moment's attention when they're fed.

And the feeding… not the meals you'd hope for, for growing children, but a kind of gruel of oats and mashed corn and whatever morsels of vegetable or meat can be gleaned, and then all of it blended down and offered in giant bottles, with no sterilisation for the teats. They feed ALL of the children this way, not just the babies. Sometimes the kids choke because they're just left in their cots, with liquid food running into them through a too-big hole, and no way of regulating the flow, so it's drink up or die… Elizabeth, it's horrific!

Back to my point: the children who were spared the respiratory disease were left in the care of two members of staff, neither of whom wanted to remain in the orphanage, because there were precious few funds coming in, and only a few children left, so they didn't think it was worth their while. So they contacted some wicked, wicked people, and SOLD the children.

You might not think they'd fetch much of a price (the lecturer told us) but even though they were stunted from life in their cots, they were classed as 'desirable' by a group of individuals I cannot bear to acknowledge as human – traffickers – because the one thing these bottle-fed children know how to do is suck.

It made my stomach churn.

And if that wasn't bad enough, the child in the study – Džesika - was shunted from country to country across Europe, before finally landing in the hands of the social workers in England, after being discovered in the house of a very rich man, who (unsuccessfully) tried to pass her off as his adopted daughter. She was eleven. She'd left the orphanage when she was seven. She'd been in his care since she was nine. The man went to jail, where the other inmates beat him to death (I couldn't help but be pleased about that).

The child and her own account of what had happened to her were duly documented and the social workers were left to decide what to do with her.

She stayed for a few months each with a number of different foster families, each of whom were unable to manage her bizarre and terrifying behaviour (which included biting herself until she bled, painting the walls with her feces and urine, alarming school teachers with graphic compositions (in perfect English) of twisted fairytales, each containing more horror than any young mind should know, elective mutism, constant thieving, and harming small animals) and sent her back from whence she came. Eventually they stopped searching for families for her, and committed her to the English care home system, which nonetheless fed, clothed and schooled her.

At 15 she disappeared, the day after she sat her GCSE exams (she had taken them a year earlier than is the norm, and yet still the results later reflected a slew of top grades) and was never seen again.

This case was held up as an example of how the very best of intentions and hard work can sometimes still prove ineffective to save the child. At various points after she was brought into England, Džesika was seen by healthcare and education professionals under the guise of 'adopted daughter', but still, no-one picked up on anything.

It was only when, in the end, a school teacher noticed a livid scar, formed of cigarette burns, on the back of the child's spine, just under her collar, that anything was even understood to be amiss.

At that point I flipped the page on the leaflet and saw the photographs they'd taken of the child once she'd been rescued. They'd blanked out the eyes with a black stripe, but this skinny girl with clenched fists (photographed in just her underwear to document the torture wrought upon her) had an incredible defiance in her posture, and dark wavy hair tumbling around her shoulders. The tilt of her chin and the shape of her mouth seemed familiar, and I felt my stomach twist as I tried to think where on earth I might know her from – or indeed HOW!

Her entire body was covered in livid bruises - clear belt-buckle shapes across the backs of her thighs; her torso a mess of scars; grazes on her knees and the palms of her hands... and Elizabeth... on her spine, just below her collar-line, those cigarette burns... they were in the shape of a flower. And I suddenly heard an echo of your voice telling me about your mysterious lodger's unusually shaped scar...

At that point I was so traumatised I ran out of the lecture and threw up in the bathroom. I need to know, Elizabeth, please find out, and tell me that this woman's scar is ANY other shape but this. And in ANY other place. I know you voiced suspicions that the woman staying with you has a 'mysterious and troubled past', as you say, but I really, really, *really* don't want this to be it.

I worry for your safety, Elizabeth. Please contact me when you receive this, if only to put my mind at ease.

Yours always,

Andrea

Toronto Star, August 14, 2012

TORONTO STAR

Tuesday August 14 2012 · thestar.com · 20% CHANCE OF SHOWERS HIGH 24C WEATHER MAP ON S16

New Information In Popović Murder

Police are now investigating the Popović family for connection to organized crime and an Eastern European human trafficking ring. Andrej Popović, aka. Anto Crncevic was wanted by INTERPOL in suspicion of child pornography, prostitution, and human trafficking. With this new information, police have re-directed their investigation into the Popovics' deaths, seeking suspects connected with organized crime. The whereabouts of the suspected lodger are still unknown, and police have issued the following statement:

"We are definitely interested in speaking to this individual, or individuals, whatever the case may be. We still don't know if they are a person of interest in the homicide, but we do suspect that they may have information pertinent to this case. In cases such as this, often times a witness is afraid to come forward for fear of retribution. If this is the case, please contact us immediately. Wherever you are cannot be safe. We can offer you protection. Please help us bring these killers to justice."

Continued on E17

INTERPOL Seeks Conspirators

The search continues for any links to what International police have called a 21st Century blight. The Popovic murders are just the most recent in what seems to be a growing concern. Organized crime from Eastern Europe making its way across the Atlantic and onto the streets of Toronto, Montreal.

DARK PLACES

ZOE ABELL

99 cents on Amazon

New Information in Popović Murder

Police are now investigating the Popović family for connections to organized crime and an Eastern European human trafficking ring. Andrej Popović, aka. Anto Crncevic was wanted by INTERPOL in suspicion of child pornography, prostitution, and human trafficking. With this new information, police have re-directed their investigation into the Popovićs' deaths, seeking suspects connected with organized crime. The whereabouts of the suspected lodger are still unknown, and police have issued the following statement:

"We are definitely interested in speaking to this individual, or individuals, whatever the case may be. We still don't know if they are a person of interest in the homicide, but we do suspect that they may have information pertinent to this case. In cases such as this, often times a witness is afraid to come forward for fear of retribution. If this is the case, please contact us immediately. Wherever you are cannot be safe. We can offer you protection. Please help us bring these killers to justice."

"Does any of this make any sense to you?" I asked. "I mean, really? How much of this can possibly be true? Can it really all be about the same person?"

Penny didn't answer. I could see her hands trembling as she read Andrea's letter. It looked like she wanted to tear it to pieces.

"She always scared me more than just a little bit," she said. "But if any of this is true – and I don't mean the bit about the demons – I may have said once or twice that Jessica's the fucking devil incarnate, but I didn't really *mean it* – then how is she not insane?"

"Are you kidding?" I asked, and I was beyond trembling. I was terrified. "Don't you see? She *is* insane. We've been living with a mad woman, Penny. If even a bit of this is true, then we might be in danger – if not from Jessica herself, then certainly from whoever might be looking for her."

Penny went pale, and then shook her head in disbelief.

"No," she said, forcing a laugh. "No, no, no. How do we know that's not just Jessica's notebook? Just a bunch of abandoned story ideas she's not gotten around to writing yet?"

I gave her a doubtful look.

"So, what do you want to do about it?" she asked me.

I flipped back through the journal. There seemed to be a couple of options.

"I say we find this doctor," I said. "And if not him, then the writer – M. Haley. She seems to be the last person – alive anyway – that Jessica spoke to before she came into our lives. Maybe she knows where to find her."

"I don't know, Helena," Penny said. "Maybe she left for a reason, you ever think of that? Maybe she's even trying to protect us. I mean, what if she caught wind of someone looking for her, and so she took off?"

"Maybe," I admitted. "But – and I know this is going to sound strange – I worry about her. Especially now. There was something about her that was so vulnerable when I took her in, and she trusted me enough to protect her. I just need to know – for myself – that she's okay."

Penny sighed. "You're as crazy as she is. Well, all right, I suppose there's a reason Al Gore invented the Internet."

"I thought it was for pictures of pussies," I suggested with a grin.

"There is a lot of porn on the Interweb," Penny agreed.

"Well, that, too," I said. "But I was referring to adorable kittens."

"I walked right into that, didn't I?"

"Yeah, well, don't take it too hard," I said, pulling her in for a hug. I was quite shaken by what the journal had revealed.

"Lemme go," she said, squirming from my grasp. "What's the name of the hospital that quack doctor works at again?"

"Arcadia Heights," I said, and we exchanged a look of surprise.

"Seriously?" she asked. "Arcadia? As in, the Countess of?"

I shrugged. "Weird."

It wasn't the last weird thing we were to encounter.

Two weeks later, Penny and I were ready to call the police. Jessica still hadn't shown up, and we'd had no success in tracking her, or anything related to her. We'd been searching the Internet, looking for Arcadia Heights or a Doctor Kenneth Howard, with no success. We both agreed that it was possible that the crazy doctor had changed the names to protect both himself and his patients, but then, he'd said from the start that the only reason he was keeping the journal at all was for insurance in case anything happened to him. What good was a journal meant to vindicate you, if all the names were pseudonymous?

Then there was the matter of these supposed women who came and took the baby and threatened the doctor. When Penny and I read through the journal again, we realized that he really never mentions them after that first time. Wasn't the whole point of the journal to lead whoever read it to the people behind the abduction?

Penny pointed out that the story of Jessica's strange birth was so far-fetched that she'd be willing to bet that the whole thing was bullshit.

We gave up trying to find Dr. Kenneth Howard, instead focusing on trying to find the writer. Again, we did an Internet search for *The Evergreen Kids*, and came up with nothing.

"What the fuck is going on here?" Penny asked no one in particular. "This book does not exist. It's not on Amazon, it's not on Goodreads, hell, I even called the publisher, and they've never heard of it, or M. Haley. But you know what's really strange?"

"What?" I asked, just as frustrated as Penny.

"I found it on eBay," she said.

"Fuck off!" I said. "Show me!"

Penny did a search on eBay for *The Evergreen Kids* and sure enough, someone was selling a first edition, signed by the author, for $150.

"Where are they?" I asked excitedly. "Contact them. There! There! Hit the *Ask Seller a Question* button.

"Says they're in the Bahamas," Penny said. "That's going to be some expensive shipping, Helena."

"Ask them where they got it," I said. "Ask them if they actually met the author."

"Well, of course they did," Penny said. "It's a signed copy."

"Please," I said. "I send signed copies of my book all over the world."

"Fair enough," Penny shrugged. "Okay, I've sent her the message. Now we wait."

Days passed, and we still hadn't been able to find any information on Kenneth Howard, Arcadia Heights, or M. Haley. In fact, the only thing we could confirm was the most recent information – the address on the envelope. The letter to Elizabeth Popović. The address was real. It existed, and was indeed the site of the double murder.

"We should call the police," I suggested.

"And say what?" Penny asked. "That we've been harbouring a fugitive for a year and a half? That she's been staying in our basement writing stories for your blog?"

"This," I said, shaking the letter in her face, "is the only real solid evidence we have. This is the only part of that journal that we can confirm is true."

Penny tore the letter from my hand.

"All we can confirm is what was in that newspaper story. *Andrej and Elizabeth Popović were found murdered in their Yorkdale home.* Anything else is just us filling in the blanks."

"She had the letter!" I exclaimed. "Why did she have the letter?"

"Yes, and supposedly, she sent that letter to a doctor we can't find any trace of!" Penny argued. "What if she's lying, Helena? What if she killed those people?"

I felt like I was going to throw up.

"All the more reason to call the police," I said, hating the sound of the words coming out of my mouth.

"What if they deserved it?" Penny asked under her breath.

"What if they didn't?" I countered.

Penny stormed out of the room, angrily. I knew she wasn't angry with me. She just didn't want to talk about it any more.

A few days later, a postcard arrived in the mail. On the front was a beautiful ocean scene, with the words Greetings from the Bahamas in large white script across the top. On the back was handwriting both Penny and I were quite familiar with.

Dearest Helena & Penelope,

By now, I'm sure you've discovered my little notebook.

If I'm right, it kept you busy long enough for me to escape unnoticed. I'm not one for long goodbyes, and I couldn't have you chasing after me. I'm afraid you're on your own, now, dear bleeders.

Did you enjoy my little tale? Have you decided yet how much is fact and how much is fiction?

Or did I make the whole thing up just to fuck with you?

There is so much history here in the Islands. So many ghosts, so many legends, so many monsters hiding in the shadows. The sun wreaks hell on my pale complexion, but it's the perfect place to write my next novel. They say that Christopher Columbus landed here and was afraid of the people he found. A savage race of people he called the Caribs. They terrified him so much that the next natives he encountered, he slaughtered or enslaved outright, assuming they were of the same tribe. I don't know how much of that is fact, or just the assembled narrative of historians, but the idea of so much carnage inspires me in ways you cannot imagine.

Like I said – there are so many ghosts in these islands.

I think I'm going to enjoy it here.

Jessica

APPENDIX: THE MISSING PAGES

Note from the Authors

After receiving Jessica's post card from the Bahamas, Helena and Penny continued to search for answers in the mysterious journal. As of this writing, they have not yet been able to find the elusive (or possibly fictional?) Dr. Kenneth Howard.

However, on searching Jessica's living area, they did come across several stashes of papers, some seeming to match the paper of the journal, others, folded up with them, were assumed nonetheless to belong with the rest of the journal.

After having read them, we have decided to include them here for your examination. Some are merely curiosities – small observations by the doctor. Mostly they are transcripts of the stories – presumably as told by the doctor's patient Margo – but attributed to the demon Raconteur.

In some cases, such as in the initial tale that piqued Helena and Penny's interest, the entire tale has not been preserved. Penny has suggested that in this case, perhaps Jessica is planning on publishing it elsewhere, and has destroyed part of it to avoid having it being used without her consent. That being said, there is something fascinating about the tale, particularly in its obsession with birth and reproduction.

A final note – all observations or comments throughout these notes have been reproduced from the missing pages, and are presumably those of Dr. Kenneth Howard, and not the authors.

Paraxenogenesis

There was something breathing in the other room.

Alice sat in the corner, knees to her chest, shaking her head, knowing it was impossible.

The rain stopped, and after what she had just witnessed, the stillness outside, and the eerie calm inside the cabin made her weary and frightened. These days she tried to avoid the quiet altogether, preferring instead to be surrounded by music or the cacophony of the city – anything to shut out the jealous thoughts that plagued her whenever she saw a baby carriage, or heard the laughter of children. At night when all was still and she lay in bed beside her husband, she could almost hear her biological clock tick-tick-ticking in her ears.

They both wanted children so badly. They tried naturally for five years, and then decided to seek medical intervention. They both went through all kinds of tests, and in the end, it was determined that the difficulty was Alice's. No one told her that she would never conceive, but the message was clear that it wasn't going to happen without the help of fertility specialists, which they couldn't afford.

Michael borrowed money from his parents for the treatment – three months of hormone injections, and then after that was unsuccessful, the fertility doctor recommended an even more aggressive dosage for a further three months. Again, nothing happened. Every month when the time came, Michael did his part, and after six months, the doctors started talking about In Vitro Fertilization, which they said they couldn't guarantee would be successful, and would be much more expensive.

About three months ago, after night after night of Alice crying herself to sleep, Michael finally told her that he didn't want to do it anymore.

"I can't stand seeing you suffer like this," he said. "I don't want us to live in constant disappointment of what we don't have, when we could be enjoying what we do have. And these dreams you keep having – these nightmares – it's not healthy."

He stroked her cheek, wiping the tears away, and tried to kiss her, but she pulled away. She'd been pulling away ever since that night, filling the ever-growing silence between them with whatever noise would shut out her grief.

The sudden silence of the cabin was maddening. It felt like an almost physical force pushing down on her, smothering her. The contrast was just too stark – not a half hour before, the air had been filled with screams and screeches, and some strange, inhuman clicking noise that sounded like the bleating of a robotic sheep. Now it was a dead calm, but behind the dripping raindrops and the furious beat of her heart, there rose a wheezing, gasping sound from behind the closed door of the bedroom.

She saw with her own eyes what happened to her husband, but still could not bring herself to believe it. No explanation could ease her mind, or make any sense of it, and nothing was going to make Michael any less dead. And yet, the breathing continued.

There are certain things the mind just doesn't have any point of reference for, and the thing that came out of the vanity mirror and grabbed Michael defied conventional thought. Even as she was screaming at the insane impossibility of the creature's very existence, her mind tried to make sense of what she was seeing and spat back two words at her: spider and teeth.

What alarmed her most was the sense of recognition she felt when she looked into its horrible eyes – huge white pools with no iris or pupil. She felt as if the thing knew her, and worse, that she'd seen it before.

After months of waking up shaking and covered in sweat, Michael insisted that she see a doctor. Her doctor suggested seeing a grief counsellor. She told her about the nightmares she was having – dreams in which she was pregnant, and gave birth to a monster that ripped her apart and then turned on her and ate her with its rows upon rows of needle-like teeth. The grief counsellor sent her to a shrink, who nodded and jotted notes as she described the thing she gave birth to as almost like a mechanical spider, part creature and part machine.

"And then it eats you," the doctor repeated back the last part of her story from her notes.

"Yes," Alice nodded. "I feel like I'm going crazy. How could I dream something so horrible? How could my mind do this to me? What does it mean?"

"Well," the doctor said, "I think that you are grieving the loss of your children, and at the same time experiencing an anger and resentment, much in the same way some women experience post-partum depression. Some women have been known to hurt their children."

Alice gave the woman a blank, unbelieving look.

"I think your mind is at war with itself, and as a defense mechanism, part of your subconscious is turning your unborn children – the children you have been unable to have – into monsters, so that the part of your mind that still longs and desires for children will find the prospect less desirable. You're trying to convince yourself that you don't want children."

The doctor prescribed a mild sedative and sent her on her way. Alice didn't feel any better at the thought that she was symbolically turning her unborn children into monsters as a way to cope with her inability to conceive, but she was glad that she didn't mention the sudden paranoia she'd been experiencing. Everywhere she went, she felt eyes on her. She thought she saw people staring at her out of the corner of her eye. She found herself checking her reflection in car mirrors, windows, puddles, trying to catch a glimpse of whoever – or whatever – was following her; spying on her.

Then one day, she was standing in front of her mirror with a pillow under her shirt and posing, seeing the pregnant version of herself that would never be, when suddenly she froze. She swore that she saw someone staring back at her from the mirror.

"I'm not crazy!" She screamed, beating her husband's chest with both fists. "There was a face, a horrible face. I saw it, Michael!"

Michael held his wife and fought back tears. The nightmares he could deal with, but if she was starting to see things when she was awake...

Suddenly Alice was obsessed with mirrors, insisting that she couldn't be around them; that she didn't trust them. So Michael indulged her, even though it broke his heart to see her falling apart. He took down the mirrors he could, and covered up the ones he couldn't, and that seemed to calm Alice down some. But he couldn't take down the mirrors everywhere, and pretty soon, Alice became afraid to leave the house. She refused to go back to the doctor, insisting that what she saw was real, and not just in her head. Any time Michael tried to calm her down, she started screaming at him, blaming him, cursing him for not giving her a baby.

Michael would have done anything to give her what she wanted, but the doctors had told them there wasn't any problem with his sperm count. When Alice screamed at him, he had to remind himself that it was the grief talking and not to respond with the truth – that the problem was with her biology, not his.

For weeks, it was nothing but screaming and crying, and strange talk about catching glimpses out of the corner of her eye of faces staring back at her out of reflections in windows, spoons; a sink full of water. Then one day, he came home and found Alice sitting in the spare bedroom – the one that would have become a nursery, but never would be – just sitting and rocking. When she saw him, she looked up at him with love for the first time in months, and reached out her hands to him. Smiling, he reached out and helped her up and into his arms.

"I'm sorry," she said, and wept into his shoulder. "I'm so sorry."

"Shh," he replied, cupping the back of her head with one strong hand and wrapping his other hand around her back and holding her tightly.

"This room," she said, "this house is killing me. This big empty house is killing me."

"Killing *us*," Michael corrected. "And I'm not ready for us to die."

"Oh, Michael, what are we going to do?"

"What do you say we rent a cabin on the coast for the weekend; get out of the city?"

Driving through the rain for hours, they listened to an audiobook that required their attention and discouraged conversation, though in truth, neither of them was really listening to it. The rhythmic swoosh-swoosh back and forth of the windshield wipers, and the droning patter of the rain mesmerized Michael, and the voice coming out the radio was merely ambience for him. Alice had her eyes closed, avoiding the glimpses of things she was desperately trying to convince herself were not real in the side mirror, or reflected in every raindrop.

They stopped at a trading post, where they could pick up the keys to the cottage and any supplies they might need. Michael said he'd take care of the rental, and could Alice pick up some drinks, snacks, and whatever else she wanted.

Alice picked out a six-pack of Heineken for Michael and a bottle of cheap red wine for her, a carton of milk and a box of cereal. She moved, trancelike, toward the sales counter, her eyes drawn inexorably toward the convex mirror to the left of the counter, wedged in between an advertising board for KOOLS cigarettes and a Budweiser clock. Something in it caught her eye – something that didn't belong. She stared at it with trembling hands clenching the few items she'd picked up, and when the silvery bubble started to ripple, she nearly dropped everything and screamed.

"Ma'am," a voice called, pulling her back to reality. She glanced at the mirror again, and saw that nothing was out of the ordinary.

"Yes, sorry," she said, putting down her purchases on the counter. "Wool-gathering, as my grandmother would have said."

"You heading on down to the cabins, I suppose?" The man said, making conversation.

Alice nodded, still a bit shaken.

"I'd recommend getting some candles or lanterns or something, if you don't already have 'em. Storms like this, sometimes we lose power."

Again, she nodded, and looked around for her husband to return.

"And we've got dry firewood for sale, too. If you weren't prepared for the wet, that is."

"Yes," Alice said.

"Ma'am?"

Alice looked up at the man, who was regarding her with a look of concern. He wore a Pabst Blue Ribbon t-shirt and had a great beard of the likes you used to only see on shut-ins or serial killers, but had suddenly become popular among the early twenties crowd. Alice didn't think it made him look gentle or sensitive, only unkempt and disheveled. She'd been wool-gathering again, lost in the messy tangles of the young man's beard.

"Ma'am?" he repeated.

"I'm fine, thank you. I'll have my husband pick up some firewood. Thank you for the suggestion."

"You sure you're all right? Do you need me to call someone?" And then in a hushed tone: "Is he taking you somewhere against your will?"

"What?" Alice asked, alarmed. "What? No!"

She shook her head like a dog drying off, in an effort to shake off whatever it was that was haunting her.

"Sorry," she said, forcing an embarrassed smile. "You've got the wrong idea, really. I've just not been well, that's all. How much for all this?

The clerk took her money and made a mental note of her face, still worried that she wasn't as fine as she'd claimed.

She could leave. She could just leave and she'd be fine. Just get in the car and drive to Canada and start a new life. Leave Michael's body – what was left of it, anyway – for the police to find, let them try to understand what happened. If she stuck around; tried to explain it, they'd lock her away.

Alice held her breath and listened to her pulse thumping in her ears. It was impossible. What was more likely was that she had some sort of episode; some sort of psychotic break, and that her mind was manufacturing some kind of monster to reconcile what she didn't want to admit – that she killed her husband. The doctor told her about how her mind had created monsters out of her unborn children. These monsters had visited her in her nightmares.

"No," Alice said to the empty room, moving her dry and pasty lips just enough to hear her own voice. "I'm not crazy. I know the difference between dreams and reality, goddammit."

Something moved in the other room, and Alice stifled a shriek.

Impossible.

Michael was dead. Whatever else had happened, whatever else she knew, she was sure that Michael was dead.

But what if he wasn't. What if he was still alive? What if he needed her help?

He had to be dead. There was

(The page is torn here, we have not been able to locate the rest.)

From the Journal of Dr. Kenneth Howard, Psy.D., M.D.

April 3, 1974

I have been furiously wracking my brain to remember all I can and write it down. I cannot bring myself to believe in demons – even though I've been given a name – The Raconteur. Aren't names supposed to have power over demons? I think I read that somewhere. Maybe it was even the Bible – didn't Jesus cast a demon named Legion into a herd of pigs?

Whoever or whatever was plaguing my patient (God rest her!) had been whispering stories in her ear for months, maybe years. And as I read back over these stories, I can almost believe that it was a demon – or demons – maybe that same Legion from the Gospels. A demon with many voices. The woman (whoever she was) said that the baby would become *The words made flesh.* I looked up the Gospel of John, and read the very first verse: "In the beginning was the Word, and the Word was with God, and the Word was God." I'm no theologian (or an expert on Christian mythology) but I understood what was being implied, and as I applied that to the strange child whose impossible birth I'd witnessed, I was filled with a mix of awe and terror.

Would this child be the embodiment of those stories that were whispered to Margo? How could one person contain all of that knowledge, all of those voices? Impossible! One tale in particular frightened me. I couldn't believe it could possibly be the coinage of my Margo's brain. What was truly frightening was what I discovered when I asked her to write it out for me...

The Magpie's Tongue

Pappy says he don't know where Mammy is. He says the wolves got her, that they ate her an' made themselves strong an' had cubs an' that Mammy is inside every cub that howls in the night when they wait an' watch from the edge of the woods. Then he laughs with his mouth, an' he chases after me, howlin' an' roarin' like a wolf near enough ready to kill me.

I don't believe him about the wolves cuz I remember the long walk, you see. The shadows was long when we set out an' long when we came back, so we was walkin' all day. When we got to a clearin' he sets himself down on the ground an' points at this big, white rock an' says 'There's your Mammy'' an' I thought she *was* the rock an I got to thinkin' that all kinds of nature can mix together like that, so when I saw a bird pickin' on a caterpillar, I thought that they would make a butterfly. Pappy tells me that I've got a heart of stone from my Mammy, deep inside my chest. Sometimes, when Pappy hollers an' screams an' beats on me, that stone heart feels heavy enough to drop right out onto the ground.

I told Jez that my Mammy was a big, white rock lyin' far, far away an' he told me that she wasn't, she was weak, an' she died bornin' me, an' *his* Mammy had died keeping the family safe from a bruin. *She* was a proper tough lady an' Pappy had been real sad when she died.

An' then one time after Pappy had been drinkin', he changed his mind an' said yes, I killt my Mammy when she was bornin' me an' I was a killer with a heart of stone an' he hadn't wanted me borned anyways. He said he only took Mammy to his bed cuz she was there an' cuz he could, but he would still rather I'd been dead than her, cuz she was good under the sheets, even if she had learned all of that with someone else, under their sheets an' not his.

Pappy an' me an' Jez live at the edge of the wilderness, an' it used to be a settlement, just a bunch of houses down a dirt path off the side of the big road. We live mostly alone now, but there was other people livin' near us before things went bad, some I can remember an' some who left before I was borned, who Jez told me about.

There was Razor, the old man who shaved his beard away every day until the pond dried up an' he couldn't see himself in the water no more. He said he would be leavin', an' then Jez told me he sharpened Razor's blade on his strop when Razor weren't lookin' an' Razor cut his neck an' bled until he died.

Then there was Mad Annie. She had her cats that all had names an' made kittens that rolled around all over the place gettin' under Pappy's feet an' makin' him curse real bad. Mad Annie gave the cats all her food an' Pappy says she took some of our food, like the meat an' fish he had been saltin' in barrels in the barn. Then, we had the real long winter after the real hot summer an' all the food was gone. Pappy killt Mad Annie's cats when she was sleepin' an' then Pappy an' Jez ate them, cuz they could. Pappy told Jez that it was retribution on Mad Annie, for bein' a liar an' a thief. An' then when she woke from her sleep, Pappy told her I'd killt her stupid cats an' she ran at me with her fingers scratchin' at my face an' spit spewin' from her mouth an' screechin' like the sick ones an' the crazies do.

An' then there was the No-Names. Jez said that the day they turned up, they wouldn't be tellin' Pappy what they was called, an' Pappy said they was runaways. An' then they said they was called Mr an' Mrs Smith, an' then it was Mr an' Mrs Jones. The lady didn't have no ring on the finger you're s'posed to be wearin' one if you're a proper lady who's wedded in the eyes of Our Lord – that's what Jez says. An' they had two children, little runts Jez called 'em. One of them had a squinty eye an' the other one was just a baby, an' it just cried all the time. Anyways, the No-Names disappeared one night an' left the baby in a box. It cried an' cried an' then the cryin' stopped. I don't know what happened to it after that.

Jez says that where the wilderness is, there used to be a proper town, with lots of people, an' cars, an' vans an' a school. I don't know what a car is, nor a van, nor a school an' so Jez draws them in the dirt with a stick. He says cars an' vans move on wheels an' don't need no horse to be pullin' them an' that they can go real fast. I don't believe him cuz he's always lyin' an' so we get into a fight an' he punches me hard in the stomach until I give up an' tell him he's right. We have a cart an' we have a horse an' it ain't got a name.

Sometimes, Jez talks to me as if he likes me, but mostly he don't. Mostly, he's away with Pappy, collectin' food from towns far over the hills where all the people have left, or they just died right there in their houses. They trap animals too, like dogs an' cats that have gone wild, an' foxes an' rabbits – there's lots of rabbits. One time, they came back with a horse that was black an' white striped all over its body. Jez says they found it in an old zoo, he says that's where animals from all round the world was kept until things went bad. Anyways, Jez tried to tame it, but it was wild an' skitterin' everywhere an' when he an' Pappy tried to make it pull the cart it kicked an' bucked as if it got stung by a hornet, an' then it turned the cart over an' went runnin' off, so Pappy shot it. He cursed an' cursed an' even Jez looked scared.

I don't go with Pappy an' Jez when they go on their trips. Jez calls 'em roadtrips, but mostly, they don't go on the roads cuz that's where all the bad people go, the ones who are sick an' crazy. Pappy knows all the shortcuts an' safe places, an' so they go there. Sometimes' they get stuck in mud an' when they get back I have to spend days cleanin' the cart an' all the clothes an' tools that got covered in dirt. Mostly, they leave home before it gets light so as nobody will know they've gone, or where they're goin'. Pappy says it's survival of the fittest, an' then he spits in the fire cuz he says Mr Darwin is blasphemous, an' Jez copies him cuz he always does. I don't remember no Mr Darwin, but Pappy always spits when he talks 'bout him. He must've done somethin' real bad.

When Pappy an' Jez are gone, I stays an' feeds the animals. We have two goats an' some hens an' a rooster. Sometimes Pappy lets the rooster go in with the hens so as they can make chicks, an' when they're big enough to make their own eggs, we kills the old hens. Pappy an' Jez breaks their necks an' then I have to pull off the feathers an' take out their innards. One time, one of them wasn't proper dead when I made the cut with the big knife an' I found something beatin' inside – Jez told me it was it's heart an' that every livin' thing has a beatin' heart inside, exceptin' me, cuz my Mammy was made of stone.

When Pappy an' Jez comes back from their trips, Pappy checks over all the animals. He ain't never happy with my work, even though I am up with the sun an' goin' to bed late from lookin' after them. One time, all the goats were covered in horse mess, an' another time the hens had run out of water. I know that I didn't do neither of those things, an' I know it was Jez doin' it so as Pappy would beat on me. He gets his special belt from under his bed an' whips me with it until I stop screamin' or if I don't scream, then he whips me with it until I start. He's got a fearful wicked temper has Pappy, but he says if I hadn't killt my Mammy, an' if she had been a proper woman, he wouldn't need to be teachin' me so hard. Sometimes, he just uses his hand – he grabs me by the wrists an' hauls me up an' smacks me one an' two an' three an' four. I don't care whether he uses the belt or his hand. I ain't got nobody to care about an' nobody cares about me so it don't matter. Pappy don't care 'bout nothin' exceptin' doin' the Lord's will, that's what he says.

When Pappy an' Jez go on their trips, I go into the wilderness. I found the town what Jez told me about, an' there ain't nobody in it, just like he says. It's just buildings, an' streets, an' broken stuff that looks like the cars an' vans what Jez drew in the dirt. I don't see as how they could even go anywhere, cuz they don't have no wheels like our cart, they's just standin' on bricks or restin' on the road, all rustin'. I found some food tins, an' they still had pictures on them. Mostly when Pappy an' Jez bring back tins they don't have nothin' on the outside to tell you what's inside, an' sometimes it's a bad surprise. *My* tins have got pictures of peaches an' pears an' a cow on them. I don't know if the cow tin has meat inside, or maybe milk. It don't matter, cuz I like both of these things.

I take the tins home, carryin' them in my skirt like I seen a lady do once. I got them home an' hid them in the space under the shed with my other things that are secret from Pappy an' Jez. I've got a black an' white feather from a magpie wing, an' some marbles I found in the stream. They're all I have that's mine, exceptin' the clothes I stand up in, an' I made them myself from sheets I took from under Pappy's bed.

We're not poor, not so as you'd think if you look at the other people passin' through. We have a house standin' in one place an' don't sleep in no tent. People think we're lucky, with all we've got. But Pappy don't want to have nothin' to do with the rearin' of me, an' so I do it myself. An' Jez is turnin' nastier the older he gets an' so I keep out of his way too.

It was Blind Adam what told me about her, the lady in the trees. Blind Adam passes through, regular-like, wavin' his stick in front of him so as he don't trip up over nothin' or walk into the streams. He's got a sister down the valley an' a daughter over near the mill. He told me he seen the lady in the trees on the other side of the wilderness where I ain't never been, an' I said he was crazy cuz his eyes ain't good for nothin' but keepin' his eyelids busy. He laughs an' tells me there are other ways of seein', like with your nose an' your ears an' your fingers. He says he could smell the smoke from a fire an' he could hear singin', an' his fingers found posies of flowers tied around the trees. An' I says she was probably scared half to death, an' she was likely singin' to make herself feel better while she was waitin' for a beatin' from her man or something. An' Blind Adam tells me no lady could sing so sweet if she was scared even less than half to death, an' he thought she was singin' cuz she was happy.

An' then Blind Adam tells me my Mammy used to sing all the time, even when Pappy an' Jez was at home, but also when they was away foragin' an' collectin' an' 'specially when she was waitin' for me to be borned. He said she was a beautiful lady, with grey eyes like the clouds when they're about ready to make a storm. An' he said that when his sight started to leave him, an' all he could see was shapes like in a real bad fog, she would let him touch her face an' run his fingers through her hair so as he could remember her better when everything went dark. An' then he asked me what colour my eyes were, an' was my hair the colour of the golden sun like my Mammy's, an' I said I don't know about my eyes cuz we ain't got no mirror an' my hair ain't never been washed so I don't know what colour it is underneath. An' then Blind Adam says it was a damned shame that I should be on my own. An' I says I wasn't, cuz there was Pappy an' Jez, an' then Blind Adam made an angry face an' said that neither of them knew anything about carin' an' lovin' an' I should get away from them soon as I could. "You need a mother," he says, an' then I saw that he was cryin', an' that made me sad. Blind Adam went as if to leave, an' then he grabbed my arm an' says "Remember the lady in the trees, she can sing real good, just like your Mammy, like she has a heart burstin' with love" an' then he does leave, swish, swish, swishin' with his stick.

An' that got me to thinkin' 'bout the lady. I ain't never smelt no smoke, nor heard no singin', nor seen no posies tied to any trees. An' so I go into the wilderness a lot, goin' past the very edge of the broken town, lookin' for the posies, sniffin' for the smoke, listenin' for the sound of a lady singin' with her heart full of love. I wonder if love feels like a full belly, or if it smells like the ground after a heavy spell of rain in a dry summer, or if it warms your skin like sunshine. An' it strikes me that I don't know what happy is neither, although I know that cryin' isn't happy, cuz it makes me remember my stone heart lyin' heavy inside.

An' then I think that Blind Adam must be happy, cuz even though he has a sister an' a daughter who lives far apart, he still walks between them, even if his days are like nights without no moon. An' so he must know what someone singin' with a heart full of love must sound like, cuz he says it was like my Mammy singin' whilst she was waitin' for me to be borned. But then I am ragin' with fire under my skin an' even my stone heart feels hot cuz she left me an' died. An' so maybe she didn't love me, an' maybe she *was* made of stone, just like Pappy says. An' so I want to find the lady in the trees an' see if Blind Adam is just an old fool with stupid thoughts an' lies comin' from his mouth. Jez says he ain't got no family, an' he just pretends. Jez says they upped an' left him when his eyes stopped workin' cuz he ain't no use to 'em any more.

An' then I think that out of all the people I knows, Blind Adam is the only one who stops an' talks to me an' doesn't make me do things for him, an' doesn't strike me with his belt, nor even his hand. An' if he was bad inside, he wouldn't rest awhile an' talk to me, no, he wouldn't never do that. So, even if he is tellin' tales about a mother an' a sister, it's maybe just to make himself feel a bit better, an' it ain't doin' nobody no harm, not one bit.

An' after all this thinkin' an' bein' tied in knots like a nest of vipers, I come to mind to go an' find the lady in the trees the very next day, cuz Pappy an' Jez are goin' on another trip. Wanderin' off whilst they're at home is a bad thing, cuz even though they don't bother with me, an' Pappy don't want nothin' to do with the rearin' of me, they always knows when I'm not around, an' it always makes for trouble like when the air gets hot an' heavy before a storm.

An' so the next day, soon as they have left, I go through the old town, cuttin' through the wilderness with my knife an' then I get to the trees, an' they're dark an' thick an' I can't see no sky, exceptin' little bits where there's a gap, like where a tree has died an' ain't got no leaves on it no more. There are animals movin' around in the brambles an' ferns, an' though I can't see 'em, I can hear 'em good enough. Blind Adam says my hearin' is gooder than his even, an' he calls me a flight animal, even though he says us humans are s'posed to be predators, huntin' an' killin' things to keep on livin'.

Then I see a wolf with her cub, layin' in a clearin' where the sun's shinin' through an' I don't know who's more feared, me or the wolves. Pappy has a dead wolf hanging on the wall in the house. He killt it an' emptied its innards an' stuffed it, an' it looks like it's going to jump right at me. Jez says it's the wolf what ate my Mammy. That's what he says an' I knows he's lyin' cuz he says a wolf killt her, then I killt her, an' Pappy an' Jez they lie so much about my Mammy they don't even know what the truth tastes like any more. Anyways, me an' the wolves, we stare at each other, an' then the mother wolf picks up the cub by its scruff an' runs away into the dark, an' I'm on my own, stuck with fear.

Then just as I get to thinkin' that when it gets dark I might be killt by a wolf anyways an' none of what's true an' what's lies will matter any more, I hears the lady singin'. An' so I creep to where the sound is comin' from an' I sees her making posies of flowers, an' she's tyin' them to the trees. An' she has a tent, better than all the tents I've seen other people usin'. An' she has a fire goin' an' she's roastin' a whole rabbit over it on a spit. I wait in the shadows, watchin' her as it gets darker an' darker until only the flames show me where she is. She goes into her tent an' lays down an' everythin' is quiet.

I creeps out bit by bit until I'm standin' by the tent an' watchin' her. She has long hair an' it's spread out over a pillow, an' even in the dark, it looks like sunlight, all gold from the flames of her fire. An' then she opens her eyes, "Hello," she says an' sits up slow, like she isn't 'fraid of me at all, like she knew I was there all the time. An' I'm standin' like I'm scared to move an' my eyes go wider an' wider an' my heart is pounding like it belonged to the hen that I was guttin' that wasn't quite dead an' I think I might be sick. She tells me not to be scared, she is happy to meet me after all these months of livin' in the woods. An' I ask her what months are, an' she tells me about days an' weeks, an' how the moon works. An' then she asks me if I am hungry or thirsty, an' would I want some soup that she could make with the rabbit, an' I say yes, that I could eat somethin' if she wants. An' everythin' she does is slow an' smooth like the river down the valley on a summer's day, an' I get to thinkin' that Blind Adam ain't so blind after all.

An' then whilst I'm sittin' there, eatin' an' watchin' the lady smilin' an' watchin' me eat, I get that hot rage inside me that makes my skin burn an' my throat go tight. She's askin' me 'bout Pappy an' Jez cuz she's seen them whippin' the horse somethin' cruel to get it to go faster an' faster, an' she's seen them trappin' animals for sport an' not for food, an' she's seen them stealin' tins from travellers who ain't got nothin' but a plastic sheet for shelter an' the clothes they're walkin' in.

An' I'm burnin' like fire cuz she says it must be hard for my Pappy to be rearin' Jez an' me without no woman to help him, an' I'm scared that she wants to meet my Pappy an' be good to him, an' make him happy an' lie with him in his bed, an' maybe lie in Jez's bed too. An' so I jumps up an' runs away, an' I ain't even finished my soup. I run an' run an' keep on runnin' until I gets home, an' I lay under the shed with my tins of food, an' my magpie feather an' my marbles but that don't make me feel better any more, not like it used to.

An' Pappy an' Jez comes back from their trip early, cuz they got chased by the militia for stealin' from their stores, but they escaped well enough an' had bottles of whiskey that Jez took before they got found out. Pappy an' Jez are fired up, an' Jez in particular cuz he fought a militia man for his gun an' knocked him out with his bare fists. Jez shows me the gun, an' his knuckles all cut an' bruised, as if I would be pleased at what he done. An' so they eat a stew that I make an' they both keep drinkin' from the bottles of whiskey like it'll disappear. An' I go to my space under the shed, hopin' that Pappy will leave me alone but knowin' that he won't. An' so I wait for Pappy to come, an' he does, an' he hates me real hard. An' Jez is watchin' Pappy drag me out from under the shed, an' he's swiggin' from his bottle an' swayin' an' laughin'. An' when Pappy has finished on me, he yells out for Jez to come an' do me, an' so he does. An' after, when Pappy an' Jez are laid out snorin' I crawl away an' get water from the stream an' wash myself all over, tryin' to get the smell of them out of my head.

An' I keep out of the way, markin' time until Pappy an' Jez go away again. They don't remember nothin' from that night an' I ain't about to tell them, in case they get a taste for it more'n they already have. An' then I am gone. I don't trust nobody, not even the lady in the trees, an' so I plan to tell her that Pappy an' Jez have upped an' left an' they ain't comin' back, so she won't feel like she ought to be fixin' Pappy an' bein' a mother to Jez. Blind Adam says she sings like she has a heart full of love, but I don't want her to have love for Pappy an' Jez, just for me.

An' so I find the lady's tent, an' she ain't there, an' I think she's gone. There ain't no fire, an' the posies tied round the trees are all brown an' wiltin'. An' cuz I ain't got nowhere to go but here, I sit in her tent, an' I wait. An' then cuz it is gettin' dark an' I am tireder than I've ever been, I lay down an' I go to sleep. An' then I wake up cuz I can smell flowers, an' the lady is standin' over me, like Pappy did when he an' Jez hated me real hard an' I get real scared an' real angry all at the same time, cuz I'm only little an' I ain't got nobody, an' nothin' happens the way it's supposed to. An' I have my knife in my hand, the one I use to cut the innards out of the chickens an' as the lady bends down, as she leans over me an' reaches out, I grab hold of her hand an' pull her down to the ground an' she is laughin' as if it is a game. I remember how Jez laughed an' laughed whilst swiggin' from the whiskey bottle, an' how Pappy laughed an' laughed when Mad Annie attacked me, an' now I'm laughin' like Pappy too.

An' as she rolls onto the ground with her hair all fanned out like skirts dryin' on a line, I grip the knife real hard an' I stab it into her like I'm guttin' one of the chickens, an' I see her eyes go all wide an' her mouth go big an' round an' she's screamin'. I pull out the knife an' she is tryin' to grab me an' I push her hands away, an' stab the knife into her again an' I feel the blade hit somethin' hard. An' then I'm on my knees an' I pull out the knife an' stab it into her some more an' I'm stronger'n her cuz of all the work I do for Pappy an' I think that I should have been the daughter of Jez's Mammy who saved them from a bruin, an' then the lady stops movin' an' everything goes quiet.

An' I sit quite still, listenin' to my breath go in an' out, an' feelin' my heart of stone poundin' inside an' I can smell somethin' like hot metal in the air. An' the owl hoots in the trees, an' the animals move through the brambles an' the ferns, an' I wait until the sun comes up until I look at the lady lyin' behind me. I see that her eyes are grey like clouds just before a storm an' that her hair is golden like the sun, an' that her blood is red like poppies an' roses.

An' I take the knife out of her chest, an' as I'm thinkin' 'bout washin' it, I see somethin' shiny inside her an' I get my water bottle an' pour the last of my water over her to get rid of the blood. An' I see somethin' white, an I'm thinkin' of the big, white stone where my Mammy is s'posed to be, an' then I think about that chicken an' its heart still beatin' in its chest. An' I think that Mammy hadn't been dead after all, an' that she *was* made of stone to leave me alone with Pappy an' Jez, an' how she must have been real weak to have no strength to keep herself safe from a little girl like me.

But mostly, I got to thinkin' that she deserves to be dead, an' how havin' a heart of stone is the only way for me to survive in this world after all.

April 3 – continued

Margo told me about this tale – a tale that frightened her so much, and whose characters got inside her head so much so that she could hear their voices. I asked her what they were like, and she told me she couldn't explain it, but that they were rough and guttural, and cruel.

I asked her if she thought she could write it down, and she came back the next day with this story, and she said that she had stayed up all night writing it.

I didn't contradict her, though I am, to this day, puzzled. The handwriting was not hers. When I first met her, I had asked her to write a little bit about herself – I find it helpful to understand what the patient's own self-narrative is in order to get to see how they see themselves.

I compared this to the story she had handed me.

My name is Margo, and I am 23 yrs old. I've been living with headaches all my life.

Pappy says he don't know where Mammy is.
He says the wolves got her, that they ate her an' made themselves strong an' had cubs an' that Mammy is inside every cub that howls in the night when they wait an' watch from the edge of the woods.

This is clearly not the same hand.
What if it's not the same mind?

Suicide Forest

It's almost twilight, the rain is falling hard, and I don't want to find what I'm looking for.

Hunched at the shadowed foot of majestic Mount Fuji, Aokigahara is a sea of trees, full of old bones.

They call it Suicide Forest.

I shiver, zipping up the red hoodie beneath my yellow plastic anorak, and check the map drawn for me by a Buddhist priest. Compasses are useless here, something to do with the magnetic properties of the volcanic rock floor, or so the locals say. There are also stories of screaming spirits, of white shapes dancing between the trees, of an ominous and menacing sense that the forest doesn't *want* you to get out.

Stay, it seems to say. *Stay and play. Forever. Let's be friends.*

"There are three kinds of people who come to Aokigahara," the priest told me, sketching out my route. "The ones who come to die, the ones who come to watch, and the ones who come looking for the lost."

"Which one am I?" I said.

"Your friend," he said, after a long period of not blinking, "is probably dead."

The priest practices from a makeshift altar in the car park, praying for the troubled souls who come here to get lost. He told me that evil spirits draw unhappy people to this place.

It sounds crazy, but I can feel them.

Determined, stubborn, I put the map back in my pocket and push on towards Ice Cave.

"I will find you, Miko," I say aloud, words echoing through the empty space. "I don't want to, but I will."

The trees crowd together conspiratorially. I pick through fallen branches and rotten logs, rocks and slippery roots, overgrown with wild mushrooms and wet hollows of moss. Strewn between the paths are grubby scraps of tape and string that hikers have trailed behind them, like Theseus unwinding his ball of twine in the labyrinth of the Minotaur.

It is the perfect place to die. Even *The Complete Suicide Manual* says so. I can see why so many people choose it as their final resting place, so dense and thick with wind-blocking trees.

It is a place for people who don't want to be found.

I almost step on a skull, half-submerged in the earth...

Aokigahara was once a popular spot for 'ubasute', the practice of carrying an infirm relative off to a mountain and leaving them there to die. In one tale, a son carries his mother uphill on his back; she stretches out her arms, catching the twigs and scattering them in their wake, so her son will be able to find the way home.

I can imagine her now, as clearly as if they were walking in front of me, her head resting on his shoulder, face wrinkled like a walnut. I can see only his back but I can tell that he is quietly angry but proud, resigned to being the one burdened with this terrible task.

"Keep going," she mouths, encouraging us both.

I pass signs emblazoned with messages like, "Consult police before you decide to die!" and "Stop! Your life is a precious gift from your parents!"

Evidence of a dozen kamikaze pilgrimages is strewn amid the dense undergrowth: weathered statues, laminated prayers, plastic flowers, mixtapes, a dog-eared paperback with a pagoda on the cover. It is rain-sodden, infested with insects.

It is one of those famous books about the great honour of sacrifice, about star-crossed lovers making pretty, embracing skeletons. It is the kind of story that says it is better to die than to live in shame.

Three miles in, I find my first body: a white, bloated carcass of middling age, spread-eagled on the ground. Scattered carelessly around his corpse are the remnants of a lost life: a briefcase, a gold ring, a liquor bottle, a pill bottle...

Further along the path a headless woman sits upright, halfway down a steep incline. Her blue blouse and jeans are perfectly preserved, and she is still wearing her slippers, but her body has been ravaged by the creatures of the wilderness.

They have taken her head, and one hand.

How is it possible that no one has come looking for her but me? And even I am really looking for someone else.

Once a year, a group of volunteers combs Suicide Forest for bodies.

Today is not that day.

Four pairs of moss-covered sandals mark the graves of an entire family, their bodies long returned to earth. Hanging above is an envelope containing photographs, one showing two small children dressed in elementary school uniforms. A blue stuffed bear is propped up nearby, missing one beady eye.

That's when I spy her.

In the small hollow of a tree several yards away, curled up like a baby on a thick bed of dead leaves, lies the body of a young woman in a soiled kimono. She rests on her knees, her arms slumped against the ground.

A long red gash runs diagonally across the right side of her pale neck, forming a congealing pool of blood in which fronds of black hair are floating.

It isn't Miko, but it might've been, once.

She wanted to come here together, to hunt for ghosts, she said.

Now she has become a spectre herself.

I recall the story told to me earlier by the priest. One day he saw a young woman staggering out of the woods, a noose still hanging around her neck. Her eyes were popped and she could hardly talk.

"She looked half-dead already," he said, "as if her soul had gone."

He took her in, fed her and wrapped her in a blanket. When she had recovered enough, the girl told him the branch had snapped.

"It is a sign," said the Priest, smiling, "that you are meant to live."

But the girl could only cry.

"I can't even kill myself properly!" she sobbed. "At least if I was dead my father would love me!"

I stare at the not-long-gone body, wrapped in silk.

Worms writhe around her embroidered cherry blossoms.

"Is someone looking for you?" I ask.

Stay, the dead girl seems to say. *Stay and play. Forever. Let's be friends.*

April 5, 1974

I am at a loss to explain where this story comes from. I'm quite certain Margo had never been to Japan. I had never heard of Aokigahara, and had to search for hours in the library to find any information about this so-called Suicide Forest. It does, in fact, exist, and that Margo wrote about it (or was it the demon, Raconteur?) begins to convince me of some otherworldly knowledge being imparted to her? How else explain this? I am beginning to frighten myself.

April 30, 1974

Getting settled in here in Arcadia. The hospital is modern enough, though some of the ideas of the staff are positively archaic. I half-expect to bear witness to an exorcism to expel the demon of homosexuality at any moment. But then, my own beliefs are crumbling, the more I consider all the things that Margo told me. Not so much in her own testimony, but in the stories she relayed to me – and I say relayed, because she claimed no ownership over them.

I asked her once if this voice of hers had a name, and she denied it. I wonder now if she were being completely honest with me. Maybe names really did have power.

She did tell me once that the voice tried to convince her that it was a spirit – an ageless spirit that, she said, "had witnessed the birth of worlds, and the whole of human history." It told her stories it thought would convince her of this. I must say, this first one I found quite amusing – it appears this Raconteur (as I am slowly beginning to make peace with calling it) is not without a sense of humor.

John Milton, You Son of a Bitch

"So do you have everything?" Lem asked, knowing his partner had a habit of forgetting things.

"I think so," Rael replied, taking an inventory of the pack he carried whenever he went on a mission. The pack was ancient, and made of the skin of a long-extinct animal from a world that no one remembered but him. It had been his charge to destroy it, after all. He remembered everything about it. He carried the burden silently.

"Did you remember the flaming sword?"

"Yes, of course. Though *why* we'd need it is beyond me. I don't expect them to give us any trouble, do you?"

"Well, it's intimidating, ennit?" Lem replied with a grin. "I mean, nobody fucks with a guy with a flaming sword do they? Nobody says *Well, you've got a flaming sword, so what? I've got a... well...*"

"What?"

"I dunno. I mean, really, what would one use against a flaming sword?"

"These creatures are primitive, Lem. All we have to do is show them our true forms and they collapse in awe and fear. The flaming sword's a bit overkill, don't you think?"

"Well, it's what the Word wants – it's kind of tradition, you know? Serpents, apples, flaming swords... the whole nine yards. Besides – better safe than sorry, I say."

"It all seems a bit dramatic, that's all," Rael sighed, and looked down at his feet. The craft that they were riding in came to an abrupt stop and hovered there, hundreds of miles above the planet, which was dark and peaceful. Azrael and Lemuel looked on in silence, waiting for the sign. They'd done this before, and while it was never certain whether they'd be needed or not, it was better to be ready to intercede than to be unprepared. Once, on another world millions of light years away, the two inhabitants that they were charged to observe had fled the garden, only to get eaten by one of the unnamed creatures that lived in the outer darkness. There was a lot of weeping and gnashing of teeth, and some other rather disgusting sounds that were not so pleasant. Azrael was to have been there with his flaming sword to first clear out the old ones that had taken up residence there, but Lemuel had wanted to stop off for a pint somewhere near Orion, and had gotten into a rather heated discussion with one of the minor Principalities about the nature of time and space. They ended up being late, and the whole experiment was ruined. Since then, their kind has been forbidden from drinking alcohol.

"Well, it may be dramatic," Lem agreed, "but you've got to admit, it is effective. Just do me a favour, will you?"

"What's that?"

"Just remember that we're there to chase them out, not kill them. I'm still hearing about that time that you decapitated that poor bastard."

"Hey, he surprised me!" Rael protested with a smirk. "He snuck up on me and surprised me!"

"Right, right," Lem relented. "Just keep the fancy swordplay to a minimum, okay?"

"Agreed. So do you think...?" Rael started, but was interrupted by a bright flash just off the horizon, followed by a sonic boom – the sound of a star falling from the sky.

"There it is," Lem sighed. "The Morning Star."

"Do you think he'll go along with it this time?" Rael asked

Lem shrugged and turned on a monitor, "Does he have a choice?"

Moments earlier, a tall, proud being stood defiantly, arms crossed, before the throne of the Word. The Seraphim were chanting relentlessly, and it was beginning to give him a headache.

"Please," he started, "can we just talk about this?" That morning he had received word that it was all beginning again, and that he was needed.

"What is there to talk about, Morning Star? This is your function. It was why you were created. Only you are strong enough to perform this task. I choose you, above all angels, to do this."

"Yes, again and again and again! And it never works! Don't You see? You give them paradise; they disobey, and things fall apart. You give them paradise; they screw it up, and things far apart. You give them paradise; they flip You the bird, and it all falls apart. It's the same every time! And who gets blamed for it all? Me, that's who!"

"You are my instrument, Morning Star. You are the first step on the road to redemption. You demonstrate to them the limits and consequences of my gift of free will. Without you, reconciliation would not be possible."

"Or necessary! I mean really – free will? *Really?* That's Your gift to them? Not such a great gift, you know? And as for me being Your instrument in redemption – try telling *them* that! I mean, do You remember how those apes depicted me? Like I was the bad guy? You give them free will, and they use it to rape each other, kill each other, turn their world into an utter cesspool, and yet *I'm* the bad guy. And don't even get me started on Milton, or that Dante fuck. I did as I was told, and I end up being known as some sadistic half-goat demon with nothing better to do than to trick people into doing shit they would have done anyway in order to have them join me for all eternity, where I'm supposed to torment them day in and day out for all time in, ahem, Hell, which, by the way, I still haven't seen. Where is this fabled Hell I'm supposed to inhabit? I mean, don't get me wrong, I wouldn't mind my own digs, but does it have to be all fire and brimstone? And another thing..."

"HOLY HOLY HOLY," the Seraphim chanted.

"Can you shut them up for a minute? I'm trying to talk to you here," Morningstar snapped.

"They serve their purpose, as do you. Please continue."

"Look, I'm just tired of being the bad guy. I don't want any Hell to rule – I'm more of a loner – I have no interest in having millions of people crash my place for an all-night S&M fest, know what I'm saying? I get queasy at the sight of pain – I'm not really the torture sort, You know? Please, I'm begging You. Take this cup from my lips – You understand that, right? I mean, what makes You think it's going to be any different this time?"

"What makes you think I want it to be different?"

"WHAT?" Morning Star yelled, surprised and angry. "You mean You *know* that it's not going to be different, and yet You keep setting up your little ant-farms, knowing full well what the result is going to be? What kind of sadistic asshole are you?"

"HOLY HOLY HOLY"

"SHUT UP!"

"Careful, Morningstar. You cannot see the full results. Those who live in the City are happier now than they have ever been."

"Compared to what? To their shitty brief lives of violence and madness and death? And now You tell me that's all part of the plan? Do the others know this? Does Azrael know that destroying his precious Earth was all part of the plan? Have You seen the way he hugs that piece of cow flesh? How do You think he'd feel if he knew of Your indifference? He cried for centuries after You made him destroy that world. He was inconsolable. Why do You think he started drinking in the first place? But You'd ask him to do it all over again, wouldn't You? I mean, if this time it all goes wrong again, You'd send him to destroy this world, too. Just wipe the slate clean, kill them all and let us angels sort it out. Well I won't be a part of it. I'm not going. I won't do it! You can't make me!"

"ENOUGH!"

And the Word spoke, and there was a great flash and a rumble that cracked the heavens, and the Morning Star fell from the sky and plummeted to the ground, throwing dust into the air and turning the sky black, blocking out the sun.

When the dust cleared, Lucifer, the Morning Star, found himself staring up at strange faces. The woman-thing reached out to touch him, and her mate stopped her, pulling her hand back.

"What is it?" she asked

"I don't know," the man said, frightened. "Let's go ask Father."

"No, wait!" Lucifer said, gasping for air. At the sound of his voice, the two newborn children of the Word were frightened and cowered away from him.

"Don't be afraid," the Morning Star spoke, words that came naturally to every angel.

"We saw you fall," the woman said, in awe, pointing to the heavens, which had gone black as soot. "From the sky."

Lucifer stood up and brushed himself off, trying to assume a form that would be least frightening to these frail, hairless creatures. He refused to be a snake this time, so he took their own form, even though it pained him to do so. When he spoke, he smiled, and tried to put them at ease. These primitive creatures, he reflected, always reacted poorly when something fell from the sky.

"Yes," he finally said calmly, "that does happen from time to time."

The couple was silent, and stared at him as he took in his surroundings. Lucifer had lost track of how many worlds the Word had created, and how many times he'd gone through the motions of crafting the downfall of His precious pets, but still, each new world amazed him. He gazed at the garden that these two had been given, and tears welled up in his eyes.

"Magnificent," he said under his breath – almost a prayer.

"What do you want, friend?" the man asked cautiously.

"Just to talk, that's all," Lucifer replied. "I just want to walk in the garden and talk with you – just like you do with Father."

"You know Father?" The woman asked. "Who are you?"

"Yes," Lucifer grimaced, "I know Father. And who I am is not important. You are Adam…"

At the sound of his name, the man looked surprised, and amazed.

"… and you, my dear, must be Lilith," Lucifer continued, smiling. He'd made this deliberate mistake before a hundred times. A thousand times. It amused him still to watch the reaction.

"I'm Eve," the woman said crossly, and then turned to her mate. "Who's Lilith, Adam?"

Adam shuffled his feet and blushed, his olive skin turning nearly purple. "No one, my dear. This man is a stranger to us, and knows nothing. There is no Lilith, only Eve." He put his arm around his mate and held her close, a nervous and uncomfortable look on his face.

Lucifer merely smiled and said, "Yes, of course. Sorry about that."

So they walked in the garden, and Adam and Eve told him the names of all the animals they passed, and Lucifer smiled and nodded politely, until they came to the tree in the middle of the garden, and here, Lucifer got very upset and anxious. He'd been in this situation before, and he was determined to change things this time. As Eve reached for a piece of the fruit of the tree, Lucifer slapped her hand and yelled at her.

"What do you think you're doing? Weren't you told not to touch this fruit?"

"Well, yes... Father told us that we couldn't eat it – but surely that doesn't apply to you. You are a guest here, and should have the best of all things... and this fruit must be special, otherwise why would Father forbid us from eating it? Here, you try some and..." At this, he slapped her hand again and screamed in frustration.

"Look, lady, I don't want your fucking fruit! Why are you so bound and determined to get yourself into shit? Weren't you told not to touch it?"

"Yes," Adam replied. "We were told that if we touched the fruit of this tree or ate of it, that we would surely die. Right, Eve?"

"Yes," Eve nodded. "Yes, that's what Father said."

Lucifer laughed, but not because he thought it was funny. He laughed because it was either laugh or cry, and laughing made him feel a bit better.

"Oh, you fools!" he laughed. "You won't surely die!"

"We won't?" Eve asked, confused.

"No!" Lucifer cried. "No, no, it's much *worse* than that! Death is *nothing* compared to what will happen to you if you eat that apple. Look, have either of you ever heard of a guy named Milton?"

They looked at him blankly, but with undertones of both fear and curiosity.

"No, of course you haven't," Lucifer sighed, shaking his head. "Never mind. Just *don't eat the fucking apple, okay?*"

Startled, they jumped at the sound of his voice, which had, for a second, become the voice of the Morning Star, terrible and powerful. He had hoped to instill fear in them; that in telling them the terrible truth, he could coerce them into compliance. Instead, he backed them into a corner, and the reaction he got was not to his liking.

"Oh, really?" Eve said angrily. "And what do you know? Why should we listen to you? For all we know, you're here to trick us!"

"What?" Lucifer gasped. "Look, I'm not the bad guy here. Do you know what will happen to you if you eat that apple? He's going to kick you out of here. I know. I've seen it happen. I've seen it happen again and again and again. I've seen it so many times, I'm sick of seeing it happen."

"No," Adam said sternly. "No, Father wouldn't do that. He loves us. We will always have the garden."

"Not if you eat that fruit, you won't."

"He's lying, Adam. He is trying to keep the fruit all for himself. He knows that if he eats the fruit he will become like Father. Come, husband. Let us eat of the fruit ourselves, and then we will become wise, like Father, and cast this stranger out."

"You've got to be kidding me!" Lucifer roared in frustration. "Do you really think that by eating a piece of fruit, you insignificant little ticks are going to become like the Word? Are you that arrogantly stupid? It's a trick! It's a test! It's a … You know what? Forget it! Do whatever the hell you want, I'm out of here. Just remember when you're telling this story later on that I tried to stop you. I'm not the bad guy here. But seriously – do yourselves a favour – don't eat the apple."

With a parting glance, Lucifer walked away out of the garden and into the outer darkness. As he walked away, he heard the unmistakable sound of an apple being bitten, followed by the angry cry of the Word echoing through the sky.

"Shit," Lucifer muttered, then disappeared into the darkness.

Hundreds of miles above, a loud alarm went off aboard a vessel containing two passengers. Azrael looked at Lemuel with disappointment and resignation and sighed:

"Here we go again."

April 30 – continued

Speculative fiction and parody, I expect, but the way that Margo told it, she seemed convinced that the voice was trying to say that he had been there. Margo said that she'd laughed, and that the voice's reaction was angry and petty, like a child throwing a tantrum. She confessed it was the first time she'd been afraid that whatever it was that had been whispering in her ear all these years might turn on her.

"I'll tell you a story," the voice told her, incensed at her laughter. "I'll tell you of a suicide – history says it was a suicide, at any rate. But I'll tell you the story. I was *there*."

The Man From Kerioth

It was never a matter of whether or not I was going to kill him; it was only a matter of *when*. Nothing in the contract specified whether or not my employers wanted me to stop the target from completing his task, and so it was up to me to decide. I watched him with his friends, and knew what he intended to do – what it would mean; how it would change things. I watched, as they told me to, outside the walls of the estate, as my target sat and ate with his friends. The smell of the food made my stomach ache and my mouth water, but I held myself in place, never stirring, only keeping my eyes on my target, as he fled the table; as if there had been some sort of disagreement or something.

Where are you going, my friend? I thought, and began sharpening my blade on a wetted stone, making slow, circular motions, almost unconsciously. My blade was an extension of my hand, and my hands had a mind of their own. They knew, perhaps even before I my conscious self did, that the crucial moment was quickly approaching. Soon I would have to decide whether to kill this man – and prevent his actions – or stand by and watch as my target set into motion a terrible injustice. Of course, I knew what my employers *really* desired – they wanted me to clean up their mess – but what they *asked* for was simply the death of this man. A semantic argument, perhaps, but this is life and death I'm talking about.

I knew nothing of this man, but I had heard of the crowd he traveled with. Some people said they were troublemakers. To others, they were heroes, and when they had hit town a week ago, they were received with celebration. So why now, I asked myself, did someone want at least one of them dead?

As a rule, I never ask an employer *why* they want the person dead – I find it easier that way, and safer, too. The less I know the healthier I'll stay. But something about this case just left a sick feeling in my stomach. Rather than ask my employers directly, I asked around town; discreetly inquiring any knowledge about the man I was hired to kill. About him, I heard very little – he came from a town called Kerioth, and he was traveling with the men who had arrived the week before, and while the other men seemed to have no money for food or wine, this man – my target – suddenly had funds aplenty. Which in itself would not be overly strange, but for the other gossip I heard: it seems that the local church groups and other religious types had been protesting this group, calling for them to be thrown out of town, especially their leader, who, to hear them talk, you'd think was the devil himself. Now there was talk in hushed tones that someone had put a contract of sorts out on him.

Ordinarily, I'd chalk this kind of think up to *none of my business* and just get on with the work that I had to do, but I slept uneasily, and had bad dreams. I just couldn't figure why anyone would want this other man dead. Everyone in town seemed to love him. Everywhere he went, crowds of people followed, hanging on his every word; wanting to touch him, wanting to talk to him and his friends.

It puzzled me, and my heart ached day and night. It aches even now, as I sit outside the window, looking in to the man and his friends, talking and drinking together, unaware that their fellowship was about to be broken by betrayal and murder.

In the end, sadly, my decision was taken from me. I had watched them for hours, watched as they retired to the yard; watched as one by one, they fell asleep out in the garden, under the moonlight. Then I, too, must have nodded off, and by the time I had awoken, it was too late for me to stop the man I was sent to kill. Already he had surrendered the man he had called *friend* to the police, who had roughly ambushed the men just before dawn, taking them by surprise. I watched as the other men scattered, then set my sights on one in particular. With rough tears in my eyes and a mixed feeling of shame and relief – shame that I had not the courage to make the decision, and relief that the burden had been taken from me – I traced my target's fevered retreat from the yard, and set into the shadows to follow him.

I caught up with him just outside of town – I had followed him for some time, and watched as he begged and pleaded with the men who'd hired him – but they just laughed at him and turned him away. Distraught, he wandered aimlessly out of town, where at last he met with a blow from the hilt of my knife. I then quickly loaded him up and rode him out to a small plot of land I knew of – a lonely place, where no one would find me in my work.

As I tied him up to an old broken tree that stood alone in the middle of the field, my normally cool and clinical heart was full of anger. As I followed him that morning, I had heard the news of what they were doing to his friend – the man he'd turned in – and I began to feel hatred. I hated him for what he'd done; I hated the men who were responsible; and I hated myself for letting it happen.

He was still unconscious from the blow to the head, but was beginning to come to. I wanted him awake, so I slapped him across the face. He awoke abruptly, and began trying to struggle against his bonds. It was no use – he was not the first man I had ever hanged.

We looked at each other in silence for a moment – he did not whimper, he did not plead, he did not even try to bribe me, though he held his blood money tightly in his clenched fist.

"God forgive me," I whispered, and kicked the mule out from under him. His eyes went wide, and his face quickly flushed with blood. My hands pulled my knife from its sheath, and plunged the blade into his stomach, tearing a hole across him and spilling his entrails at his feet, all over the thirty pieces of silver that had fallen from his clutched hand.

"Judas, you traitorous son of a bitch, *why?*" I screamed at his dying face.

I got no answer; only the echoing laughter of a nearby murder of crows.

I turned and walked away, never looking back.

April 30 – continued

I have no idea how to interpret that. Who is the narrator? Surely not the demon Raconteur. Why would he share this tale with Margo. What was he trying to convince her of? So much of this is a mystery.

September 5, 2001

I had buried this journal deep, as well as the secrets it held, for years. I had something of a breakdown, convinced that of the existence of demons and other stranger things.

Physician, heal thyself!

I could not even see the paranoia until I nearly lost everything, least of all, my mind.

Everything was going so well. Until *she* showed up at the hospital. This young woman is so strange, and has such a vivid imagination. We know so little about her – most of her medical history is either lost or incomplete – and when I ask her to tell me about herself, she tells me a different story every time.

Then there was the incident with a patient, and a fire, and I another patient was complaining about being terrified of this young woman, and I began to start travelling down a dangerous path of thought again for the first time in years.

I was afraid of this young woman. This *Jessica B. Bell*. And I wasn't the only one. Mary, the poor woman with the self-mutilation issues, she's convinced that Jessica is the devil. And then there's this note I found when we were cleaning out the room of the young unfortunate woman who set fire to herself.

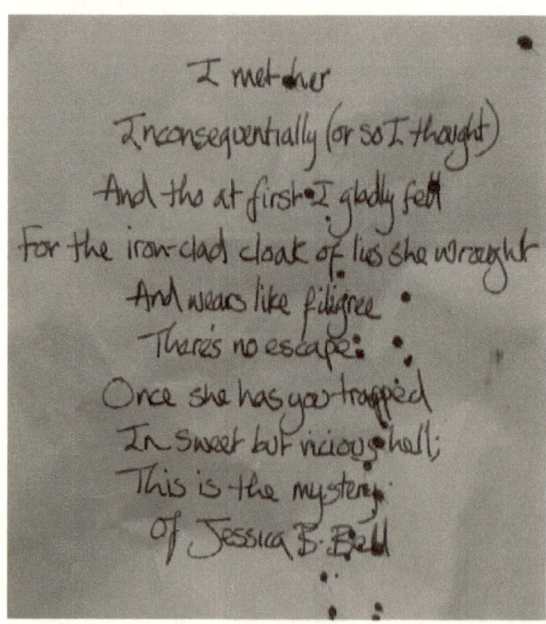

I Stayed
Because I knew not what I did
As vulnerable as she seemed
'Twas all an act, and now I cannot rid
Myself of this obsession.
My mind is overcast.
She was never mine to keep
She captured ME, and well—
Now, how deeply I abhor
That Jessica B. Bell

I purged
I gouged her from my skin and mind
She laughed like thunder,
Eyes sparking, sent me blind
Yet even through the blood
I reached for her.
I am undone now
Writhing, I can hear the knell:
She smiled and I fell dead.
I still ♥ Jessica B. Bell

It's not uncommon for romances, however ill-advised, to develop between patients. This poem concerns me, though. It seems to be written by someone obsessed with *Jessica*, and perhaps not in a completely benign manner.

November 3, 2006

I found another of Margo's stories. *They were not written by some demon, goddammit!* I didn't spend years and thousands of dollars just to throw away everything I accomplished in therapy! Reading them is difficult. As much as I know, I know, *I KNOW* that Margo wrote them, that Margo was brilliant but troubled, and that if she had only been able to conquer her demons (not demons, *psychosis, dammit!*) that she could have been a terribly successful storyteller, I cannot reconcile the sweet, gentle woman with a story like this one that I just found, and have forced myself not to throw in the fire.

There is a House in New Orleans

The la Croix mansion sat abandoned long before I moved to New Orleans. Squatting on the edge of the encroaching swamplands, its once proud pillars were swathed with Spanish moss, the tumbling porch tinted green, seasick with moss and decay. I heard rumors about it – even in my rundown room in the Quartier Française. Several young girls went out to the swamps for an illicit rendezvous and never came back. Nothing – no bodies, no ransom note – ever appeared. It seemed the swamp swallowed them forever.

I hadn't been out to the swamps – spending most of my days smoking too much and working too little on the screenplay I promised by the end of the month. Some people found the heat oppressive, maybe that was it. But in a city so rich in history and culture, so full of inspiration for tales of the grotesque and the beautiful, I thought there was no way I could fail. I was adrift in a sea of unfamiliar sights and sounds – the melodic French of the people around me, the gritty, dirty building where I lived. I spoke the poorest schoolboy French, but the rent was cheap and God knows I could use the money. The jazz that wafted through the air, borne along with the smells of the bakeries and patisseries, lured me out to walk the cobblestone streets. I passed dark men playing for pennies and the hedges around Jackson Square where women lured men of all colors and incomes, the fancy cafés with their gleaming silver, the Garden District where everything was clean and brass-buttoned doormen guarded the portals to a world as far removed from mine as the moon that gazed down on the Mississippi.

I was walking along the river one night, watching the moonlight touch the tips of the waves with its silver fingers. I saw lights. I thought it was a ship, coming in late to the docks, but I realized it was coming from the la Croix place. I didn't think I had a chance in hell at hiring a car, but, when I walked towards the more brightly lit streets, deciding to try my luck, one pulled up smoothly beside me. I hadn't seen the headlights.

"Need a lift, mister?" the cabbie asked with the slight slur that made the New Orleans accent so attractive.

"I want to go see the la Croix place," I said, waiting for him to spit and drive away.

"Sure, mister, I can take you there for cheap," he said.

I stared a moment before I slid into the back of the car, drinking in the smells of stale cigarette smoke and perfume of previous passengers. The ride passed in silence; my cabbie was not one to chatter. He was right – in terms of distance the place was close – but I felt we travelled back years when he pulled up at the end of the overgrown drive. You could still see that the place had "good bones," but I could see where the swamp was beginning to take over. I wondered how long before the whole place vanished.

"I guess you can't go much closer," I didn't expect an answer.

"Closer, mister?" Without waiting for my response, the cabbie drove right up the drive – past the twisted, rusting gates set in moss-furred stone – until we reached the front door. I pictured the la Croix women in their French silk dresses stepping lightly down those stairs to meet their carriage.

"Get out and take a look, if you want, mister," the cabbie's voice sounded excited.

I wondered if it was fear – the adrenaline of standing in the place where four girls vanished. I stepped out of the car, listening to the swamp. I thought it would be quieter outside the city, but a different cacophony of noises met my ears. I turned to ask the cabbie when the la Croix family left it when everything went dark.

❧

"Not exactly what I ordered," the voice was accompanied by an awareness of a sharp pain in my wrists and ankles.

My eyes adjusted to the dim lighting as I regained consciousness. Everything blurred. I got the impression we were in a wood-paneled dining room with a vaulted ceiling and a chandelier. Statues lined the walls. I blinked. Not statues. Four young women hung there, the same as I – bound wrists hanging from a hook securely in the wall, legs spread and tied to rings in the floor. The girls each had a large tub beneath their feet. Except for the parts that marked them as female, no skin remained. The buckets caught the blood. My eyes skittered around the room to the long table laid for one. The chandelier glittered off the cutlery and the china, sparkling in the golden wine.

I smelled the tang of sweat, coppery blood, and freshly butchered meat. It reminded me of the slaughterhouses along the docks and I leaned over, retching. The bile that spewed down my chest splashed into the bucket beneath my feet. I heard the drip-drip of blood and I turned my head to see a tall, lean man at the body of the girl to my left. Her once luscious hair, chocolate with hints of red and gold, clung to her fleshless face and nearly hid her empty eye sockets. The man worked steadily; his knife flashed as he cut off a slab from the girl's side, cleaving to her ribs. His hands were bare and I saw the dark red slowly glove them as he cut.

"The meat is best at this age," he said.

His voice was conversational as he laid the slab of meat down onto a silver platter, wreathed with greens like any fine restaurant. He rolled the cart to the table and sat down, not bothering to wipe the gore from his fingers. He cut a thin slice and took a bite; blood dribbled down his colorless lips.

"She wanted to die first," he gazed at the girl across from me.

Rust colored blood soaked her blonde hair. Little flesh remained on her torso and I looked away from the bite marks visible on the skin she still had, hanging down over the empty cage of her ribs.

"But her screams were so lovely," he grinned a red smile at me. "That I just couldn't let her go."

He hummed, conducting an imaginary symphony with fork and knife. I heard a noise and lifted my head, ears straining past the dripping and the scrape of cutlery on china. The door burst open and my cabbie strode in, dragging a girl. There were marks on her skin that made me sick, no scrap of clothing shielded her poor, tormented body. The pale man at the table smiled broadly and licked his thin lips, coating them with blood from his appetizer.

The girl's hoarse sobbing rose to screams that echoed off the walls. I don't know if the ropes came loose or if the hook couldn't bear a man's weight but I jerked involuntarily and landed on the floor, my feet tangled in the bucket meant for my blood. I started towards the girl but the pale man, with a leer at me, picked up his thin knife and carved straight between the struggling girl's breasts and down through her stomach. I knew it was too late as the white tablecloth turned red. I staggered out into the swamp. They found me three days later.

I can still hear the screaming.

June 2, 2007

I woke up from a nightmare. In my dream, a strange, disfigured imp sat on my chest while I slept and whispered horrible stories to me, giving me nightmares. This creature fed on my fear. I wonder if this is what it was like for Margo. At least I'm not hearing voices. I'm not paranoid. I have little pills that take care of all that. Mostly.

Body Snatchers

I stretched my arms back behind my head, feeling the joints pop as my sleepy muscles sprang back into use after long hours of inactivity. There was a lingering feeling of wine around the edges of my mind, blurring my peripherals and making the room seem cosy and bright.

Susie grinned and threw a cushion in my direction, both of us laughing as it walloped softly into my face and plopped down into my lap. I scooped it up and threw it back half-heartedly, rolling my eyes as I missed and it glanced off her onto the floor.

"Go on with you", she said. "You were meant to be gone hours ago. I'm not sure you shouldn't just stay the night at this point."

I hemmed and hawed, but decided that the idea of waking up early when she left for work (I thanked my lucky stars again that my job didn't require Saturday shifts) with a muzzy head and no clean clothes was singularly unattractive, and that I'd rather make the twenty minute cycle-ride home, even though it was 3am.

The evening had been planned for ages – her crazy shifts and my need to keep stepping in with family conspiring together to deny us of more than swift phone calls or snatched conversations in passing at the netball courts (neither of us willing to give up the game to spend time together – why, when we could play and chat?). This night was a long-awaited indulgence, and we'd clasped each minute greedily.

We began with grocery shopping, preferring to wander the supermarket aisles discussing what we'd cook, as a prelude to the whole night. Take-away was fun, and good in its place, but we wanted our meal to reflect the time we planned to share – a lovingly prepared, purposefully made, delicious meal accompanied by fine wine (alright, fine-ish) and deep, indulgent conversation.

Giddy with the freedom of the evening, we'd giggled our way through the checkout queue before returning to her house to make use of her ample kitchen; vast, glittering expanses of marble and a terribly fancy 'kitchen island' (did I mention she has to work Saturdays?) showing off the perfect decor and pots of fresh herbs at the windowsills.

Priorities: enormous wine glasses brought out before the bags were even unpacked, and we solemnly observed the glorious pop and glug as the bottle was opened and its golden nectar decanted, simmering with fragrant, intoxicating notes.

Glittering utensils flashed like our conversation as we chopped and prepared our rainbow of food. We talked like affected 1950s housewives, had pirate-style knife fights and somehow both ended up with vegetable peelings down our necks and in our hair.

The meal itself was incredible, and eventually we staggered, stuffed with fresh flavour and ready for slaughter (or slumber) to the lounge, where the bright sofa awaited with open arms to cradle us as we continued to talk. The pace became somnolent and the tone buzzed low, like sun-drugged honeybees, as sleep threatened to overtake us. Then one of us remembered the dessert, and we both squealed with delight, leaping up to run helter-skelter back to the kitchen to locate bowls and spoons and ice-cream.

Late-night-fright TV accompanied the frozen sweetness of chocolate salted-caramel (topped with hot popcorn, for good measure) and we chuckled our way through several increasingly bad horror shorts. We turned the sound down to continue chatting when a documentary about body-snatchers came on, inspired to begin a flight of fancy about Halloween costumes when we saw their ridiculous tall hats and masked faces.

The night had drawn on, our conversation becoming more and more disjointed (yet still deeply meaningful, and laden with intent) as time went by, culminating with my stretch, and the incredibly half-assed cushion-fight.

"Much's I hate to love you and make you leave me," she said "If you aren't going to stay, could you make the going rather quick, because my brain's about to fall out of my head from tiredness, and I have to maintain at least a passable pretence of a competent professional, tomorrow morning…"

"You're such a charmer," I retorted "All sweetness and light until I rebuff your overnight advances and then I'm out and back on the streets quicker than you can blink"

The next cushion was thrown with more force, and the next, as I gathered my bags and chattels together, making a big show of weathering the onslaught.

There were no drawn-out goodbyes – we'd see one another again (fleetingly) before the week was out – and I was quickly on my way, wheels purring across the damp tarmac as I glided through pools of effulgent, acid orange poured out by the street lights.

The woods lay ahead, and a decision; to cut through and save myself several miles, or to stick to the streets and pedal the extra. I could feel my bed beckoning, telling me that no-one would be out at half-past three in the morning in the middle of the woodland, and I bumped my bike off the road onto the cycle path and left the light behind me, entering a chill avenue redolent with the smell of old leaves.

I barely noticed the mist until I cycled out into the large field around which the woods had been planted so many hundreds of years ago, when this was common grazing ground. It had collected, like a fog-machine gone berserk and unstoppable. My field of vision narrowed to mere metres, and I slowed to a crawl, watching the ghostly cone of my front light become visible in its entirety, the flashing red from my rear light dancing behind me.

I shuddered and wished I could speed up, suddenly wishing I'd not watched the documentary, swearing I could see the tall, cone-hatted, blank-masked body-snatchers just beyond my field of vision, cloaked in swirling mist, prompted by my fevered imagination and lack of sleep.

A little further down the path, circling it, blocking my way and closing in behind, the cone-hatted figures solidified and began walking towards me...

January 1, 2012

This is the year I write my memoirs. I've retired, and what else do I have to do? I've put the past away, and maybe now that I'm removed from it, I can look at it objectively. Who knows? Maybe I can sort through all this and make a story out of it.

October 17, 2014

Still no memoirs. Went back to work on a part-time basis. Figured I'll do more good there than sitting at home waiting to die. Funniest thing. I haven't been in private practice for forty years, but I keep getting phone messages from my old service. Seems someone named Helena is trying to track me down. Isn't that funny? Seems to me my Margo told me a story about a Helena once.

Showtime

"You want to explain to me what the fuck Helena's problem is?"

"Maybe the fact that you're calling her 'Helena'?"

"The fuck am I calling her *The Mistrix*. This over-the-top theatrical stuff should be for the punters only."

"Jesus, Grave," Kirstoff looked up from the longknife he was cleaning. "What's crawled up your ass tonight?"

Grave slammed the trailer door behind him. When it bounced open he slammed it again and held it shut until the magnet lock took. "See? This whole setup's a joke."

"Get Bruce to fix the door if it bothers you that much."

"It's not the damn door."

"What is it, then?"

"That little 'talk' Helena wanted to have with me after the show?"

"Yeah?"

"We're not dangerous enough, apparently. She wants us to put in a countdown."

"A countdown to what?"

Grave sighed and threw himself on the patched couch. "To the nulgrav switching off. The fight has to be done by the end of the countdown or we're smeared across the set."

"Ok, we could do that."

"Oh, that's not the best bit."

"Go on."

Grave rubbed his face. "We don't get to know how long the countdown will be for until we get out there."

"Ah."

"Fuck it all," Grave leant forward, clutching his hair. "Screw her. I mean, really. Not dangerous enough? You nearly took my arm off tonight."

"Yeah, sorry about that," Kirstoff said, running his oil cloth down his blade again.

Grave shook his head, rubbing the bandage. "It's fine, medic glued it up in a second, it's not a problem. But where does she get off with this crap?"

Kirstoff shrugged and rose to stash the knife in a locker under the couch. "She's thinks nulgrav takes the danger away."

"Ok, so we're not going to fall and smear our brains across the ring like the trapeze or necrobats, but surely the sharpened knives and live ammunition make up for it? The Fools don't even use weapons and she says we lack edge?"

Kirstoff went to the refrigeration unit and pulled out two bottles. "The Games always want nulgrav performers if you want out."

"They do background checks."

Kirstoff held up his bottle with a sour grin. "To doing something you love for no pay, a shitty trailer and a ringmaster that likes bile and bones."

Grave clinked his bottle to his partner's. "I wouldn't leave you anyway, you old sod. She'd probably have you put down."

"Steady," Kirstoff said.

Grave took a swig and scowled at the bottle. "Energy drink? Where's the beer?"

"If you think I'm driving the whole way to Metropiline on my own you can think again, lad. And don't even begin to think about taking any of *that* either," he continued as Grave pulled a tin from his pocket.

"Aw, come on, man. 'Shit' doesn't even begin to cover today."

"So, suck it up. No Bliss before driving."

Grave muttered and shoved the tin back in his pocket and tried to make himself relax. He tapped the tin again, aching for a dab, but Kristoff glared. He sighed and tried to stretch the aches away. "I wish you'd let me tell her, you know. About what we really think. She asks *me* in for these talks. Don't you think she might listen?"

"She asks *you* in for the talks because she's hoping you'll give her an excuse to make our act the next DeathCut."

"Hey," Grave sat up. "Not fair."

"It's right there in the contract. Insubordination is instant dismissal. And she'd give anything to get rid of nulgrav performers."

"Audiences want nulgrav, I don't care what artistic notions of hers are being offended."

"Well you should. Are we locked down?"

Grave sighed and leaned back again, glaring at the trailer ceiling. "I locked the trunk earlier. We should be fine if that door holds."

"I'm serious, you know Grave," Kristoff said as he took the empty bottles to the disposal. "You don't want to rub her up the wrong way."

"I promise I won't get us fired," Grave muttered as he dropped himself into the passenger seat.

"It's not getting fired I'm worried about," Kristoff murmured as he brushed past Grave to strap himself into the driving seat. "Not with a DeathCut due."

"Relax, Kristoff," he replied, climbing into the passenger seat. "She's not asked us to change our death scene. The DeathCut's not us."

"No one ever knows who it's going to be," Kristoff said as the technician truck in front of their trailer started its engine.

"How can that be true? How do they work it into their act?"

"They don't."

Grave frowned. "It's improv?"

"Something like that."

"Oh, come on. I saw the last one on the banned feeds. You're telling me that Jessik girl didn't know about those explosives? That's way too dangerous."

"That's kind of the point."

"Don't be daft. They could have *really* killed her."

"Grave…it did."

"What?"

"Five years ago almost to the day," Kristoff said as the truck ahead pulled away and he starting the trailer's engine. "Last time we did Metropiline, the tour before you joined."

"She actually died? It wasn't just rumour for the punters?"

Kristoff shook his head as they pulled out of their parking bay and followed the truck.

"Well… it was an accident, then," Grave fumbled. "And why these things should be rehearsed."

"No one gets to know in advance if their act if getting cut. That's the point. It keeps everyone on their toes and makes the Metropiline performances the best, as well as the ones with the most bets. The tickets go for thousands."

"How can she get away with that?"

"Well, think about it. What are we? Drop outs, ex-cons, the homeless and the disfigured… people with no future apart from what she gives us. No on cares what happens to us on her stage. So, let's just not give her an excuse to make us the next 'improv'. Deal?"

Grave searched Kirstoff's face for any sign he was kidding and felt a little cold when he couldn't.

Grave's shoulders were even more bunched after hours behind the trailer's wheel heading down the tunnels to Metropiline. He put the trailer into park when they'd finally arrive at the show ground outside the city and leant forward to peer out the windscreen at the tangle of buildings in the valley. Some towered over others, their twisted architecture distorted further by the scatter of window lights, making them look like iridescent deep sea creatures. Networks of walkways were illuminated in blues and reds like a series of chemical arteries, pumping electric blood around in the dark. He sat and stared for a long moment, the lights smeared on the inside of his eyelids with every blink, wondering what it must be like living in a city that never saw the sun.

It took Kristoff prodding him to make him realise they had company.

"Serene?"

The woman's pale smile widened as she gestured back out the trailer door. "You are summoned."

"What, again? Hasn't your mother got better things to do?"

Serene just smiled wider and lead the way out of the trailer. Grave coughed as he clambered down into the thick air.

"Great, isn't it? Smells like home."

"Do you know how long we'll be here?" Grave said as he followed Serene across the industrial lot carved out of the naked rock above the city. The illumination from the troupe's floodlights made the dust flash in the air and Serene look insubstantial and bloodless.

"It's not so bad down here. At least you won't need radiation shots for a while." She threw him a grin over her shoulder. "The Throne's parked up over there," she said, waving between the cranes that were powering up near the tent wagon. "Come find me when she's done with you. I've got some wine in my trailer."

She melted off into the dark and Grave turned the other way. He wove amongst the techs and performers rushing between trailers, prop vans and set transports, wondering what Helena could possibly want now. The Throne would have been easy enough to find even without the black limousine parked outside. Its own set of red floodlights bathed the silver trailer in a blood-like sheen and puddled scarlet on the pitted ground in every direction. Grave went up to the door and waited whilst a security guard almost as big as the trailer talked into a wrist-comm before opening the door.

As soon as the Throne's door shut behind him it was like Metropiline, the Cirque and the rest of the world no longer existed. The soundproofing shut out the clamour of the troupe setting up and the filtered air smelt of rosewater rather than oil and dust. Grave shifted from one foot to another on the thick carpet, glancing around the sitting area, wishing he'd thought to run a comb through his hair and change his t-shirt.

"Grave? Is that you? Come through, if you please."

He swallowed and followed the voice into the next room, pacing through the lush furnishings more suited to a penthouse apartment at the top of a space-scraper than a trailer in a Cirque troupe. Helena was stood at a wide window in her office, watching the cranes lift the bundled miles of black and red polytarb off the tent-wagon. The lumbering of the machinery and the swarming of the tech and stagehands played out in eerie silence, the only audible sound the ice clinking in her glass.

Finally, she turned. "Grave."

"Mistrix."

A corner of her pale mouth twitched. Her eyes flickered behind the tinted lenses of her glasses. Grave wondered again how she had come on the same twelve-hour drive as him and yet not even one hair had slipped from her white ringlets and tried to decide if she looked more or less creepy without her stage make up.

"This is your first Metropiline show, isn't it?"

"Yeah."

"I always like to give my home crowd a little... more, you know?"

"I think I do."

Her smile froze a moment and she stood there with the crystal tumbler pressed against her cheek, unblinking gaze fixed on his. Then let out a soft laugh, coming round the desk to lean against it. "You've never seen an audience like a Metropiline audience. They're the most and deserve the most." Grave opened his mouth but thought of Kirstoff and closed it again. She drained her drink, still watching him, then opened a drawer in her desk and pulled out a silver canister with a vaguely familiar logo on the brushed metal. She placed it on the tabletop and tapped it with a red fingernail. "A little something extra. For your act."

"What is it?"

"Oh come now, don't you recognise it? This is the real deal, direct from the source. Or do you need a dab?"

"That's Bliss?"

She nodded, pink eyes glancing at him over the top of her glasses. "Pure. Thought it was add a little zing to your big finale. The people won't have to just imagine your 'blessing from the gods'."

"What exactly are your suggesting, Mistrix?"

"Come, come. I thought you were brighter than this. The smoke effects. Let's make it more than smoke."

"You want me to put Bliss, no, *pure* Bliss, in our smoke canisters?"

"Do you need to sit down? You look pale."

"Helena," Grave stammered, saw her fingers tighten on her glass and her eyes harden. "*Mistrix*, I can't... I mean... it's not safe."

"I didn't take you for an unadventurous soul, Grave. Especially as you are so intimately acquainted with this substance."

"I..." His mouth dried up. He swallowed, tried again. "Ok, I used to deal but... Mistrix, you can't predict how a vaporized dose will affect people."

"You need to learn to live a little," she said, eyes never leaving his. "And the residents of the Under City, well... let's just say we're used to living it large."

She tossed the canister to him. It was cold and very heavy. "How much is in here?"

"More than enough for all your little smoke bombs, I'd say. All of them, mind. I will know if you scrimp, my boy."

"Mistrix," Grave said, meeting her eye and not letting himself flinch. "This could kill people."

"If you don't do it, I will. Then I shall be forced to reflect on your commitment." She tutted and shook her head. "I really thought you cared about yours and Kristoff's future more." Grave knuckles ached as he gripped the canister. Helena glided back to her bar and poured herself another drink. "I think we're done. Good luck, Grave. Make me proud."

"You know talking about my mother all the time is a real turn off?" Serene muttered as she sipped her wine.

"Did you not hear what I said?"

Serene shrugged as she put down her glass and picked her whetstone back up. "So the audience gets a little high. Big deal."

"You don't understand... you need to start low. Build up a tolerance. I've been doing this for years but even I've never dabbed the pure stuff and I've definitely never breathed it. It could make people flip out... seriously flip out, mind, if not giving them brain bleeds on the spot. And not just the punters."

"Grave, relax. Why do you think she ordered in all those resp films?"

"What resp films?"

Serene sighed, gesturing out her trailer window. "Check with props. We picked up a whole new stock two cities ago. Clear ones so the punters can't even see. The troupe won't be affected."

"I don't think you're getting this. We could *kill people.*"

"Sounds like fun," Serene said, her throwing star zinging as she sharpened it.

"Serene."

"Grave," Serene snapped, pressing a finger to his lips. "This is getting boring now."

Grave blinked at her, swallowing. "Kristoff told me that that girl, Jessik, died... really died... the last time you were here."

She shrugged again and held her throwing star up to the lamp, checking the edge. "Our show is dangerous. It's part of the thrill. It's what our audience want."

"I thought it was just hype and marketing."

"Some of it is. But the most convincing lies are the ones with a grain of truth. Most of the troupe are junkies or convicts. We give them a better life than in Detention Blocks but no one ever said there was no risk. It's all in the contract. Or were you high when you signed yours?"

Grave chewed his lip, choosing not to remember that day. "Have punters ever died?"

Serene tapped her chin with her star, looking like she was sincerely trying to remember. "No. We've lost a limb or two."

"Kirstoff seems... scared."

"Honey, look," she said, putting a hand on his cheek. She smelt like metal. "I'm sorry if you managed to convince yourself it was rumour or fake or whatever...but that's what we are. The Cirque de Noir. We are the dark. And people love it."

"You believe that?"

Serene smiled. "I know it. Now give them what they want. Mother knows what she's doing."

Grave's heart thundered against his ribs as he peered out the gap in the curtain. The velvet was getting sweaty under his palm. The stands groaned as they filled with hundreds of people, their excited chatter dense in the air. Some were in costumes, spattered in fake blood or wearing masks or carrying fake weapons. He even saw one young lad, underground-pale with pink eyes and white hair like Helena, trotting along after his father in a home-made replica of Grave's own gladiator costume. His grip on the curtain tightened.

The clamour of a thousand people settling in seats and rustling refreshment packs hushed as the lights dimmed. After a suitably unnerving pause, a single spotlight lit the centre of the ring and music filled the air. It was the same intro piece they'd played the whole tour but this time it made his stomach lurch.

As the recorded drums reached a crescendo, a figure stepped into the light, at first glance walking on air. A closer look at the way she moved, however, revealed a crosswire under her stilettos. The light flashed off the red metal trim on her top hat and tailcoat. Cheers rang out and the Mistrix lifted an arm in the air with a flourish, white ringlets bouncing as she swept forward in a bow low enough to press her nose against her PVC-clad knees.

Her smile was painted on in crimson and even at this distance he could see her eyes flash behind the tinted glasses. Her artificially amplified voice rang out around the arena, but the words of welcome swam in and out of meaning. He watched her like she was in a dream as she strolled back and forth on the wire, the spotlight igniting micro charges in the air as it followed her so it looked like her body was trailing red fire.

"Shout and sing and scream, ladies and gentlemen. Remember, we aim to please as well as kill."

Another thunder of applause went round the arena as she bowed again and the spotlight vanished, plunging the ring into blackness. The Fools pushed past him to take up position for their marionette number, black and white stage make up looking ghastly in the backstage UV. By the time the lights came up again, he was alone in the wings with the knowledge that they were one act closer to his own like a stone in his belly.

He watched the performances in a daze until Kristoff came and collared him as Serene's knife-throwing was winding up. He helped his partner retrieve their baffles, foils and weapons, feeling like he was moving through water. Then they stood waiting for their entrance with Grave trying to control his breathing. Kristoff prodded him in the bicep.

"Keep it together," he whispered and handed him a resp film.

"Kristoff," Grave begged, but then the lights had gone again and Serene was pushing past him, sweaty and grinning, with the chorus of cheers and catcalls following her.

"Knock 'em dead, Grave," she whispered in his ear and kissed him on the cheek. Her smile looked strange in the darklight.

Grave shook himself as their own intro music started. He felt blood thunder in his temples as he followed Kristoff onto the ring, activating his night vision contact lenses with a couple of heavy blinks. His hand shook as he slid the resp film over his mouth and nose, feeling the sticky film take and taking a few deep breaths to make sure oxygen was filtering through properly. The clamber frames, trussed up to look like piles of rock and Roman ruins, rose soundlessly out of the stage floor and he let his body take him through the motions of locking the baffles and smoke canisters in place. Then he was clambering up into position just as the music built up and the ripple of the nulgrav activating went through his belly. He felt his weight leave him and tightened his grip on the frame, sweat breaking out all over his skin.

The lights went up and he drew his sword, staring at Kristoff across the set, the murderous glare he'd worn so many times masking the fact that he felt like his heart was trying to smash through his ribs. On screens suspended from the tent frame red numbers flashed up and started counting down. He blinked to try and keep the numbers in focus, forcing himself to think about the routine and how they were doing to do everything before zero.

Kristoff glanced one at the screen then nodded and lifted his sword on cue. Grave kicked off towards him, soaring through the air and raising his own weapon to engage. His speed took Kristoff by surprise a couple of times, needing adjustment from them both to avoid undignified tailspins. Sweat gathered on his skin and as droplets in the air as he launched himself again and again from one bit of the set to another, dodging, swinging, shouting whilst constantly checking Kristoff's counter-attacks to try and guess what he was going to change next to get all his moves in. Fake blood from the capsules in his palms and wrist guards burst on cue, leaving trails of crimson in the air and the audience gasped and cheered in all the right places.

Finally, the music cut and he was squatting on a tumble of polyfoam masonry, panting and glaring at Kristoff as he glared back at him, grimed in fake blood and dust. They both glanced at the countdown and his spirit climbed up one rung when he saw they were on schedule. The crowd was hushed as the lights dimmed to a deep rose like sunset. He gathered himself for his spring across the void to land the 'killing' blow that would win him the favour of the gods, who would then shower the scene with burst of gold confetti and silver smoke. But just as he was about to leap, the music changed. The melody lowered and sharpened just as lights flashed above them and the sound of simulated thunder rocked the air. Grave glanced at Kristoff to see confusion creasing his brow as the fake lightening flashed again.

"Stage, what the hell is happening?" Grave muttered, tapping his earpiece but no one answered. The thunder rolled once more and the countdown on the screens was replaced by the scrolling word *MASKS*.

The stands were shrouded in shadow but he could hear the shuffling of a thousand people shifting in their seats and could make out them pulling things over their faces when there was a crack and a hiss the air was filled with smoke.

"*Stage,*" he hissed but was cut off as a minty smell filled his senses and his throat closed. He coughed, swallowed air, felt his head start to spin. He groped at his resp film and froze as his fingers found puncture holes just below his nose. The thunder, lightning and music filled his ears and tangled themselves in his brain. His vision swam and heat swamped him from his skin inwards.

He blinked, trying to focus on Kristoff who was pawing at his own resp film, eyes widening and body wracked with great panicky breaths. Grave tried to call his partner's name but his croak was drowned in the thunder and the smoke. He closed his eyes and tried to calm but colours flashed on the inside of his eyelids and he heard a voice from far away crying out. He thought it might be his own until he forced his eyes open and saw Kristoff hurtling towards him, sword ready and face twisted with rage and terror.

Grave lifted his sword just in time. The clang of the weapons meeting sent electricity through his muscles and he yelled and fought back as Kristoff rained down blows.

"You did this," Kritstoff yelled, bloodshot eyes streaming.

"No," Grave rasped. "Helena - "

"It's your fault. You pissed her off."

"No," Grave tried to cry again, but his throat was dry and his breath wouldn't catch. The air flashed black and white around them, the smoke choking and clawing, the music bursting in his ears. He scrambled over the clamber frames, kicking through the air even though his couldn't see where he was going, Kristoff's blade slicing the air around him. The numbers from the screens melted and swirled at the edges of his vision and his blood was like static in his veins.

He kicked off the set again but Kristoff managed to get a stronger launch, reeling towards Grave as he tried to spin away. Metal seared through his side. His own howl echoed in the caverns of his ears and the blood he left behind in the air blurred in and out of focus until it was all he could see.

Blinking he managed to bring the top of a column into focus and made a grab to swing himself around. His partner came over the top, swiping madly. Grave got his sword between them and it shuddered with Kristoff's blows. The metal heaved and shivered as he clung there under Kristoff's assault, terror becoming a solid thing in his bones.

His awareness warped and his grip loosened. He watched his hands lose their grip and drifted backwards, leaving his sword embedded in the set. Kristoff, face twisted with fury and spattered in gore, lifted his sword with a yell. Grave tried to rope together enough control to grab his sword back but his muscles weren't answering. Kristoff's sword came down just as the lights went up and the gravity reactivated. Grave watched Kristoff, the column and the zero flashing on the screens shrink away like they were falling and not him.

He didn't feel himself land. There was crunching and splitting somewhere far, far away but he watched reality spin away like dust in a cyclone and felt some part of him smile as his spirit soared on the feeling. He couldn't tell if his eyes were open or shut. He swam amongst agony and confusion like they were waters in a river, gliding past but not penetrating, until, finally, a white face appeared somewhere above him. The only thing he saw clearly were the red lips, like a wound, widening into a grin.

"Now *that's* a finale," Helena said before she and everything else melted away.

ABOUT THE AUTHORS

Helena Hann-Basquiat dabbles in whatever she can get her hands into just to say that she has.

She's written cookbooks, ten volumes of horrible poetry that she bound herself in leather she tanned poorly from cows she raised herself, and then slaughtered because she was bored with farming.

Some people attribute the invention of the Ampersand to her, but she has never made that claim herself.

She was completely self-educated in a private institute in the Catskills where she majored in Pop Culture and Unpopular Music. She wrote her doctorate thesis on the films of John Hughes, and awarded herself a doctorate, though it's not generally recognized.

Most recently, Helena published Memoirs of a Dilettante Volume One, and is currently preparing Volume Two for publication.

Find more Helena at HelenaHB.com or follow her on Twitter @hhbasquiat

J. S. Collyer is a Science Fiction, Fantasy and Horror writer who has just released her first novel, 'Zero', a SciFi epic set in the not-to-distant future about one crew's struggles through a web of politics, deceit and revolution.

'Zero: An Orbit Novel' now available for Kindle and as paperback from Amazon.

http://jcollyer.wordpress.com.

Facebook: www.facebook.com/jscollyer

Twitter: @JexShinigami

Michelle Poston Combs is a blogger who lives in the Midwest with her husband and her youngest son. She is at the precipice of learning to live with an empty nest which she finds both terrifying and exhilarating.

Her blog, (http://www.rubbershoesinhell.com) is where she writes about topics ranging from awkward conversations with strangers to learning how to overcome being an adult child of a narcissist. Her work has appeared in numerous blogs including The Huffington Post.

She programs computers to pay the bills and counters this soul-sucking endeavor by writing her observations on life, menopause, anxiety and marriage

Freya McMillan has been writing on the dark side since she was a little girl. She spent many an enjoyable hour subjecting imaginary boarding school chums to calamitous events that never had a happy ending. For her, the boarding school japes of Enid Blyton were far too tame. These days, you can find Freya on trains, in coffee shops and on park benches, scribbling in a notebook or tapping away at a keyboard, dreaming up the weird, the dark and the disturbing. She loves the immediacy of flash fiction, but is committing her energies to a novel - with a dark theme, of course. You can find her blogging at http://freyawrites.com/, on Facebook (Freya McMillan) and on Twitter (@freyathewriter). She won the 2014 Dirty Goggles Blog Hop for her diesel punk entry 'The Silencer' and she has also been published in the September 2014 edition of The Woven Tale Press. Further work is also due to be published in a collection produced by the Pankhearst Press in 2014/15.

Hayley Morgan is a writer and creative layabout, a cat-lady-in-waiting and l'enfant terrible. Born and raised in the Black Country, Tolkien's inspiration for Mordor, she was first published at 12 in a book about the Internet. Hayley was an actress and gymnast and once performed as Scar in a high school dance club production of The Lion King, but she was more often found playing Monkey Island in her darkened bedroom with the dial-up modem that nearly bankrupted her family, listening to Tori Amos and Fiona Apple and writing weird stories about freak shows and space colonies. In her 20s she lived in Brighton and London and after going to one too many parties, managed to worm her way into the world of media, freelancing for queer magazines and working in film PR. She later worked as a bookseller and joined Cat Cooper at Elfin Productions as a Creative Associate. Hayley has recently finished her first novel, Heathens, the first in a trilogy to be published this century, and is soon to launch an interactive online literary magazine, Fiction Crowd. Claims to fame include meeting a serial killer, writing a (dreadful, truly dreadful) sex column and puking in front of Amy Winehouse.

Lizzi Rogers is English (first and foremost) and takes great pride in writing with all her words in full-on, technicolour, extra-added-'u's form. Her main goal, in writing, is to make you think, or feel, or otherwise walk away with a bemused expression on your face, and the single utterance "Damnnn!" the only thing left to say. She is dedicated to living life in Silver Linings, leaving a trail of glitterbombs and fairy-stones behind her, and In Real (as On Page) if she doesn't know a word, she'll make one up.

Hannah Sears: Born and raised in the land of ten-gallon hats, tall hair, and taller tales, Hannah has been making up stories as far back as she can remember, although she didn't start writing them down until later.

Geography's never been her strong point, so she decided to migrate North to New England to pursue an MFA in Creative Writing. When she's not finding ways to sneak movie quotes and country song lyrics into daily conversation, or buried under a pile of second year graduate student homework (or snow!), she can occasionally be found writing fiction at http://secondstaronther.wordpress.com/ (Vers Les Etoiles).

Cover designed by **Hastywords**. For more of her artwork and writing, visit http://hastywords.wordpress.com/

And what of **Jessica B. Bell**?
Look for VISCERA, a collection of strange tales, including the complete *Paraxenogenesis,* from Sirens Call Publications sometime in 2015.